Dakota
Love

• • • • •

Suzanne Drentlaw Hellman

ACCENT BOOKS

Accent Books™ is an imprint of Chariot Family Publishing
a division of David C. Cook Publishing Co.
David C. Cook Publishing Co., Elgin, Illinois 60120
David C. Cook Publishing Co., Weston, Ontario
Nova Distribution Ltd., Newton Abbot, England

DAKOTA LOVE
©1992 by Suzanne Drentlaw Hellman

Cover design by Turnbaugh & Associates
Cover Illustration by Kevin Bielfus
First Printing, 1992
Printed in the United States of America
96 95 94 93 92 5 4 3 2 1

Library of Congress Catalog Card Number 91-73263
ISBN 0-78140-945-4

Dedicated to my Norwegian grandma, Myrtle,
and my Scotch-Irish grandma, Margaret.
Thanks to Sally for believing, and Berit,
for her help with the Norwegian language.

Chapter 1

Marry him? Had she heard him correctly?

Hannah Campbell stared into the too handsome face of Erik Nelsson. How could he possibly want to marry *her*?

The perfect mouth showed perfect teeth in a smile that was trying hard not to break into a laugh. Hannah realized her own mouth was hanging open and closed it quickly, turning a bright shade of crimson.

The vivid blue eyes were friendly, not mocking, which reassured her a little. Whatever he was doing, he was not intending to have his bit of fun at her expense.

Yet she didn't know what to think. Why should Erik Nelsson want to marry her? She was definitely no beauty. Mousey brown hair. Too tall. Too thin. Too old— good heavens! She was twenty-five, and even in this region of few single women, she hadn't received one proposal. Now, out of the blue, the best looking man she'd ever laid eyes on was asking to marry her.

She'd never even spoken to Mr. Nelsson, not more than a polite "Good morning" in church or in her father's store. Now here he stood, hat in hand, waiting for her to say something.

Hannah began to realize how much time was passing. Men were hitching teams to wagons, women were packing away food and folding cloths that had been used for ground covers. Children continued to chase each other through the tall grass, not ready to declare the church picnic over.

Just to their left was the gently sloping, grass-covered bank of the Red River of the North. In the opposite direction, the sun was low in the sky, the clouds showing that pink tint that promised to blossom into a spectacular prairie sunset.

She located his three children, whom she knew by sight but not name. The oldest, a girl of about twelve, sat under a tree talking with a small group of friends. A boy of eight or so was just tackling a somewhat larger boy. The chubby three-year-old daughter ran and squealed with a small boy.

Hannah turned to face him again. "Why?"

"Vy?"

"Why would you ask me such a thing? I hardly know you."

"Vell. . . ." He hesitated.

Hannah suspected that he was not entirely comfortable with this turn in the conversation.

"Becoss I need a vife," he said at last. "Marta, my vife, has been gone over nine monts. A fever," he added, in explanation. "Tings haf not been easy for us vitout her."

That she could believe. She'd noticed in church several weeks earlier that his children were growing out of their clothing and had thought of offering to do some sewing for them. Not knowing them very well, she'd discarded her good intention.

"I know dis is sudden, and I understand vy you may not agree. I hope you vill."

"Why me?" Surely there were other women—younger, prettier women—who would be eager to marry such a man. She could think of two off the top of her head.

Those incredible eyes—eyes that rivaled the scorching, shimmering blue of a summer sky—searched out hers.

"God knows I need a vife. I asked Him to show me. Den I asked da pastor who uff da girls and vidows vere devoted to Yesus. I asked Mrs. Schneider to tell me who vas bote nice, and good at cooking and sewing."

Mrs. Schneider was very old. She was also sharp as a tack, and known to be a dedicated Christian.

"Da names Hannah Campbell and Yenny Smit vere on bote lists. So I vatch. I see you pray in da church. I see you mind your papa in his store. Today I see you holding dat baby. And I taste your cookies! Yenny Smit, she does not look so healty, so I ask you."

How flattering. Proposed to for her good health and her cookies.

Mr. Nelsson's speech, which Hannah sensed had not been easy for him to make, made sense of an incident that had puzzled her earlier. She had been holding Julia Johnson's baby, talking to him, letting the small hand tug on her braid. She'd felt she was being watched, and had turned to see Erik Nelsson gazing at her. Olaf Krueger was talking to him, pointing to her. The turquoise eyes had moved to a cookie, minus one bite, in his brawny hand, then back to her. Her face had felt a bit warm, and she'd turned away.

Clara Pederson, standing nearby, had turned away, too, from watching him, to cover her giggle with a fluttering hand. "He's looking at us! Oh, Hannah! Have you ever seen such a handsome man? And a widower, too! Oooh! I wonder if he liked my pie?"

At the time she'd been annoyed by Clara's gushing. Couldn't she see beyond a pair of unbelievable eyes and broad shoulders? Yet Hannah knew there was a touch of hypocrisy lurking within her. For all her high ideals, she was a little weak-kneed herself.

And now here he was, asking to marry her!

Clearly he'd meant no offense by sharing his process of selection. And she had asked.

He stood, toying with the brim of his hat, looking at the ground between his feet. Then once again he looked up.

"It is getting to da point," he said, "dat if I don't haf some help vit da children, I vill haf to send dem back to my aunt in Norvay."

Hannah could sympathize with his plight, but it wasn't much of a basis for marriage.

"You are serious, then, in this . . . suggestion?" She was reluctant to use the word proposal.

"Ya. Kvite serious." He seemed taken aback by her question, perhaps a bit offended that she doubted his sincerity.

"Do you require an immediate response, or may I have time to think it over?"

"Oh, ya. You may haf time. Not too much time. I am leafing Fargo soon. Going vest to claim a homestead."

"Where?" This put things in a different light.

"I tink near da Sheyenne River." He replaced his hat on his head and parted with, "I vill come to da store."

Hannah walked away, too, to join her parents at their wagon. Papa had the team already harnessed up and Mama had the food loaded.

Margaret Campbell was a short, plump woman with graying red hair and jade green eyes. She was bubbly and always moving, and it was hard to imagine her as Hannah's mother. Jacob Campbell, on the other hand, was tall, thin, quiet. Brown hair, gray eyes. Unimpressive.

"What did Mr. Nelsson want, dear?" Margaret asked.

Hannah gave a noncommittal shrug. "Oatmeal cookies."

Margaret Campbell's face, which normally wore either a cheerful smile or a pretty pout, fell. Obviously she'd been hoping for greater things.

"Well," she said, trying to make the best of it, "I suppose he doesn't get much home cooking." An idea brought the curve back to her lips. "We should invite them to dinner."

"No!" Hannah interrupted quickly. It would be like her mother to do just that.

* * *

The next afternoon Hannah walked out of her house. Her steps led her beyond her father's store to the path along the bank overlooking a bend of the river. The April weather was warm. A profusion of wildflowers bloomed in the grass. She sat on a rock, letting her bonnet dangle idly by the strings. Few boats traveled up and down the river; the only one in sight at the moment was one loaded with boxes and barrels. Probably taking supplies down river to Grand Forks.

She had decided yesterday not to accept Erik Nelsson's proposal. Now she wasn't so sure. He was probably her last chance. Two times before she'd had proposals, both back in Wisconsin. The first was from Herb Taylor, thirty years her senior and two inches shorter. The other was from George Anderson, a well-known drunk who refused to set foot inside of a church. Now Erik Nelsson wanted to marry her. Who would've thought?

The fanciful, girlish part of her wanted him to want to marry her for herself. Who she was, what she thought. Just because he wanted to be near her. The practical, unromantic side of her knew just how silly and unlikely that was.

A gust of wind blew the light blue calico skirt around her legs, and the dust it raised migrated directly into her eyes. She should have her bonnet on, she knew, but she had given up that vanity years ago. Now she wasn't nearly so careful about protecting her hair and skin as her mother thought she should be.

So should she wait, insisting on the love she wanted, or should she accept what life offered? Had she read too much poetry? too much Shakespeare? Should she put away the last of her "knight in shining armor" dreams? Was there even such a thing as love?

Hannah sighed. Yes, there was. She knew her father lived and breathed for her mother, but that didn't compromise his faith. He was obedient to the Lord—the single most important thing Hannah insisted on in a husband. Apparently Mr. Nelsson met that part of her qualifications.

What should she do? Her parents wouldn't live forever. She had no other family she knew well enough to want to turn to. She didn't want to spend her days alone.

She supposed she could contrive to marry a hunter or farmer, or even a soldier now that the train went all the way to Fort Abraham Lincoln. But that would put her in the same dilemma she was in now, only with a different face proposing the preposterous situation. On the other hand, marrying a soldier would offer some degree of safety, living in or near a fort. But that was no more of a reason to marry than was compassion for Erik Nelsson's motherless children!

Oh, it was so confusing! No closer to a decision, Hannah walked home.

Her body helped in the store, set the table, sat down to supper, but her mind continued to ponder the question. She could do much worse than Erik Nelsson. All the single women—and probably some of the married ones—would be livid with jealousy. That was not an effect she was seeking, but it was nonetheless true. Were they all right? Was she crazy to hesitate?

She did want to help the children. Who would choose to

10

see a family separated? Yet she could not picture years of marriage to a man who saw her as a convenience—a baby-sitter, housekeeper, cook, laundress.

It would be nice not to be alone. It would be nice to have a family of her own.

Wait! Hannah suddenly realized that she was going about this all wrong. *The question isn't "Should I or shouldn't I?" It's not even "Do I want to or do I not want to?" The question is, "What do You want me to do, Lord?"*

But how to know?

"What is the matter with you, Hannah?" Margaret asked, bringing Hannah back to supper-table reality with a jolt. "You've been quiet as a mouse all day."

Guiltily Hannah took a bite of food.

"Poor Maggie's had to carry on the entire conversation by herself," Jacob put in, winking at his daughter over his fork.

Silently she blessed him for diverting her mother's question.

"It's an art I've had to learn," Margaret countered smoothly. "We'd never have any noise in this house if I left all the talking to you. The only time you string two words together is when you're teasing me about talking too much."

"Soup's good," Jacob said, his gray eyes crinkling at the corners.

Margaret laughed pleasantly at his little joke, then resumed her cheerful chatter.

Hannah gave a sigh of relief. She wasn't up to small talk. Any attempt to answer would only confirm her mother's suspicions.

* * *

Later that evening Hannah sat out on the porch swing behind the store. There was only a quarter moon, but there were stars beyond counting. From the town came the

11

sounds of laughter, a piano, horses. Occasionally there was also the noise of breaking glass or gunfire. Most men in Fargo were armed, as well as some of the women. Quiet and peace might be expected from the merchants and farmers, but not from the hunters, trappers, and outlaws that seasoned the town's population. Fargo was the only spot of civilization around for miles, and the footloose type came in regularly to kick up their heels.

Hannah was used to the noises . Her father had tired of cobbled streets and gaslights when she was quite small. They'd left Philadelphia in '53 for Wisconsin, but soon that was too tame for Jacob Campbell. It had been a state since '48 and was filling with people—people who built roads and schools and had nothing more exciting to talk about than how much milk their cows produced. Jacob Campbell wanted the men who sat by the stove in his store to tell stories of Indian fights, blizzards, hunting, trapping, mining, and vast stretches of land unoccupied by white men.

Margaret had convinced him to stay in Wisconsin long enough to give Hannah the opportunities of a good education and a good marriage. The education she received—the marriage he gave up on when his daughter turned twenty-two.

One evening he'd gotten out a map and selected a lonely looking, semi-inhabited spot not too many years distant from the railroad—Fargo, on the west side of the Red River. He'd told Margaret to pack, and there had been no disuading him.

When they arrived in '71, Fargo wasn't even really a town yet. But sitting where the coming railroad would cross the biggest river between Minneapolis and Fort Abraham Lincoln, it inevitably would grow. Now, three years later, the trading post was a real store in yet another small town, complete with a school, roads, a building for the church, and even a depot. But Jacob had his wish—rugged men talking around his stove, exciting his imagination.

Hannah tipped back her head to lean against the wooden back of the swing staring into the blackness of the star-studded sky. What did God want of her? To marry him?

How would she feel about that? If she knew, beyond a doubt, that that was what she *should* do, how would that make her feel? She faced the truth. What kept her from seeing herself in the role of Mrs. Erik Nelsson was her appearance. How could a man so beautiful that he didn't seem mortal be truly happy with her? Despite what her mother said to the contrary, Hannah knew she was not pretty. Her absence of suitors confirmed her opinion.

The screen opened. Her father was briefly visible in the light from the house before he stepped into the shadows and shut the door. He leaned his long frame against the railing.

"What's wrong?"

His question didn't surprise her. He had always seen her more clearly than her mother—their personalities were quite alike. But this was not something to discuss with one's father. Or was it?

"What do you know of Erik Nelsson?"

Jacob joined her on the swing. "Saw you speaking to him yesterday at the picnic. Did he say anything unkind?"

"No, Papa." Not intentionally.

"Handsome lad. You're not mooning over what you can't have, are you? Disgracing me by flirting?"

She laughed shortly. They both knew that was not in Hannah's character.

"No, Papa. I was just wondering what you know of him . . . what is said of him."

"What are you getting at, lass?"

"He wants to marry me."

Jacob sat up straight. "That doesn't please you?"

"It could. But I don't know him. I don't know what God

13

would have me do. What do you think?"

He patted her hand. "I think you do me proud, Hannah. Not many girls care for the opinion of either their father or their Lord. They marry the first handsome face or thick wallet that comes along.

"As to Erik Nelsson—" Jacob paused, thinking. "He seems to be a good man—hard-working, cares for his family, goes to church. The pastor thinks well of him. As far as I know, he is respected. I think he would be good to you. On the practical side, I have no idea of his financial situation. The children appear to be well-fed, so I would presume he's not a pauper. But I doubt he's wealthy, or he most likely wouldn't have dragged his family out here to the edge of nowhere.

"Hannah, how do you feel about marriage—to anyone, I mean? The Bible says it's better not to. Could you be happy to remain unmarried?"

"I'm not sure, Papa. I don't like the thought of living alone."

"When your mother and I die, you could go to Quebec and live with my brother Ralph or one of your cousins. I'm not a rich man, but you would not be completely dependent."

Hannah shook her head. "It isn't only a question of where I would live or with whom. Even if all I ever do is raise someone else's children to know the Lord and serve Him, I'd have more of a purpose than sitting in Uncle Ralph's parlor doing needlepoint."

"I believe you've just answered your own question."

She drew a shaky breath. He was right, and the implication terrified her. "I guess so," she said.

"So what else is wrong? You don't sound too satisfied with your decision." Jacob shifted more comfortably on the swing, content, for the moment, to listen to the night.

Hannah knew he was going nowhere until he got some answers.

"How can you understand, Papa? He didn't . . . he wasn't . . . oh, never mind."

Jacob chuckled. "I gather he didn't sweep you off your feet?"

"Suffice to say his proposal left a bit to be desired. I guess that's understandable."

"Why do you say that?"

"To him I'm only a baby-sitter. A housekeeper."

"What makes you so sure?"

"He said as much. Besides, I'm. . . ." Her voice dropped to a miserable whisper. " . . . I'm ugly."

Jacob lifted her chin, more to establish contact than to see her in the dark. "Do you really believe that?"

"M-hm." It was an affirmative noise.

"You are the spittin' image of my grandmother, Hannah, and she was a handsome woman. One of Glasgow society's darlings."

Her father would never lie to her. Affection must be biasing his opinions.

"I'm too skinny," she protested.

"Not skinny. Slender. Some men like that."

Thank goodness for the darkness that hid her furious blush.

"I'm too tall," she persisted.

"Perhaps you were too tall for that Taylor chap back in Wisconsin, but you're not too tall for Nelsson."

Hannah was argued out. So she wasn't as ugly as a mud fence. She was still not pretty enough for Erik Nelsson.

"Did he say why he asked you? There are several other eligible women in town. He must have had reason to choose you."

She knew her father was trying to make her feel better by pointing out that this was not a decision a man reached lightly. Unfortunately, it also reminded her that everyone else would be wondering the same thing. Why would *he*

15

marry *her?* Well, she just wouldn't let them know about it, then, until the deed was done.

"I understand," she said, "that the competition between Jenny Smith and me was quite keen. The honor was swayed in my favor by Jenny's tired look and my cookies."

Jacob roared with laughter, slapping his leg.

Hannah couldn't help but see the humor of the situation, and her soft giggle joined in.

Margaret peeked around the edge of the door. "What's going on out here? A party I wasn't invited to?"

In the faint light from the door, Hannah could see her father's nod, instructing her to tell.

"Mother, first I want you to *promise* me that you won't breathe a word of this to anyone. That goes for you, too, Papa."

"Sounds serious," Margaret commented. "I promise."

"I'm getting married."

Her mother stood in a stunned silence for about three seconds, then words came in a torrent. "Who? When? Why didn't you tell me?" She frowned. "And why is it to be a secret? Come inside and tell me everything!"

Soon they were in the kitchen with tea heating.

"Who?" Margaret repeated, prompting a full explanation.

"Erik Nelsson."

"Erik Nelsson? That tall, blond man with the three . . . But you said he wanted cookies!"

Hannah slumped her cheek against her fist, her elbow propped in a most unladylike fashion on the tabletop. "That is precisely what he wants. A cook. A baby-sitter."

Her mother, the pretty belle of Philadelphia, could never understand marrying a man who wasn't hopelessly, stupidly in love. Hannah went on to answer the other questions. "When, I don't know. Why I didn't tell you is because I've only just decided. And it's to be a secret because I want it to be." Mama wouldn't understand that,

16

either. "No parties, no receptions. Understand? Promise?"

"Promise, yes. Understand? Certainly not!"

"There is one other thing I haven't told you yet."

They both looked at her, waiting.

"He's not staying in Fargo."

Chapter 2

On Tuesday morning, Hannah was cleaning in the store. Margaret was stocking canned goods on a shelf, and Jacob was muttering about his inventory, hoping the train from Minneapolis would come soon.

Erik Nelsson walked through the doorway and paused briefly. He removed his hat, looked about until he located Hannah, and moved toward her.

She panicked, watching him approach. She knew he was handsome, but the memory paled next to the reality. It had only been two days since they'd spoken. She needed more time!

"Haf you had time to tink, Miss Hannah?"

She felt she would choke on her own tongue before she could get it to work, and only nodded. Nervously, she wiped her clammy hands on her apron.

Her eyes focused on a button of his shirt. She was too

much of a coward to look into his face. "Mr. Nelsson, I don't think it would be such a good idea. You don't know me well enough." Her eyes had not remained still, and at this point, she caught his expression. The clenched jaw. The glimmer of injured pride. A multitude of thoughts, pictures like fragments of glass, spun in her mind.

His children stood outside; she could see them through the window. The oldest two appeared to be quarrelling. The youngest stood, looking lost and forlorn, the wind blowing her hair. Her thumb was in her mouth. Hannah wanted to take the little girl in her arms. An image came of this child on a ship on a long journey, sent to a great aunt she probably did not know, losing her father so soon after losing her mother.

Hannah suddenly realized how hard it must have been for him to ask her in the first place. It couldn't be easy to ask a virtual stranger such a thing, facing this very possibility of rejection, hoping to keep his children. He must love them very much.

And he *had* complimented her. No, her eyes were not limpid pools, her teeth were not pearls. He was not pining away from unrequited love. But he was trusting her with the physical and spiritual well-being of his children, the most important thing to him. And why shouldn't he have asked around about her? It felt good knowing that she had praise and respect of other community members. Not that she felt she particularly deserved it.

All these thoughts flashed through Hannah's mind in an instant. Her voice was amazingly strong when she met his eyes squarely. "Forgive me, Mr. Nelsson, for being a coward."

The blue, blue eyes searched, questioned.

"I am honored." She paused, not knowing what else to say, then simply said, "Yes."

"Ya?"

20

"Yes, Mr. Nelsson. I will marry you, if that is what you still want."

A ghost of a smile. A glimpse of teeth.

The die was cast. Fear suddenly wrapped itself around her lungs, sending her gaze skittering to the shelf, to the floor. Back to his face when he spoke.

"I should speak vit your father, ya?"

"He already knows."

The smile deepened at the admission that hers had not been a spontaneous, emotional decision.

"But I would thank you for asking his permission." It showed proper respect.

He started to move in Jacob Campbell's direction.

"Mr. Nelsson?" She stopped him. "I would request one favor, if I am not asking too much."

He waited.

"I don't want you to tell anyone else."

The golden brow arched higher.

How could she explain? She couldn't tell him how she feared the ridicule of the townspeople. Their astonishment. The crushed hoped of not a few. Plain Jane, shy Hannah Campbell, marrying walking, breathing poetry! She couldn't bear the unasked questions, the shock, the disappointment on his behalf—or theirs.

She groped for a plausible reason, and, finding none, lamely said, "I just don't want anyone to know."

"I vill tell only my children and da Yohannsons."

"Thank you." He must think her a lunatic. She was surprised he hadn't changed his mind.

"Dere are tings ve must speak uff. After I speak vit your father?"

"Of course. Why don't you and the children have dinner with us? That would give us opportunity." It was about that time of day, and it would keep her from being seen publicly in his company.

21

"Dat vould be good, tank you, if you are sure it is all right vit your parents."

"I'm certain they will enjoy the chance to get to know you better." *Before you take me away from them,* she added silently. At least her ability to properly connect words into sentences had returned, along with her manners.

Within minutes, Jacob had turned over the "closed" sign in the store window and Margaret had called the children in. They were seated around the big table, and Margaret had placed cold chicken, potato salad, bread, butter, pickles, and a cake on it.

Jacob said the blessing, then began loading plates.

"What a lovely family." He smiled at Mr. Nelsson's murmured "Tank you," and handed the first plate to the oldest girl. "And your name is?"

His question brought home to all of them the abnormality of the situation. Hannah was going to marry this man, and they didn't even know the names of his children.

"I'm sorry," Mr. Nelsson apologized for his oversight. "Dis is my daughter Eleesabett. She is tvelf."

She was wearing a dress of lilac calico, which made her eyes look violet. Her hair was a darker shade than the others, the color of honey, or taffy.

"Dis," he rubbed his knuckles on the pale head next to him, "is Yon. He is nine."

John, in profile, was a small duplicate of his father. His ripe-wheat hair, however, was as straight as his father's was wavy.

Erik's gaze turned fondly to the little girl on his other side. She was chubby, with huge blue eyes and very light hair which hung in loose curls. "Dis is Charity. She is tree. And she is a citissen!" He meant she was the only one of them born in America.

"How long have you been in this country?" Margaret asked. The plates were all full, and Margaret lifted her fork to start eating.

Following her cue, the children dug in, tasting everything to decide what to eat first.

"Almost four years," Erik replied before taking a bite.

"You speak very good English for such a short time."

He swallowed. "Again, tank you. Da food is very good. Tank you for inviting us to eat vit you."

To Hannah, this exchange of compliments was beginning to sound overdone. Perhaps she was being too easily irritated. She wished the meal and small talk were over already.

It went quickly enough. Thanks to Margaret, there were no uncomfortable stalls in conversation. She went on about how happy she was to finally have grandchildren. She asked each of them questions, what their interests were, how they liked Fargo. She asked Mr. Nelsson about their train trip west, and volunteered the information that they'd come out from Wisconsin three years before.

"Now." The word said nothing, but meant everything. Jacob pushed away his dessert plate and leaned back in his chair, his long hand wrapped around his coffee cup. "When is the big day?"

The blue eyes flicked to Hannah. "I vas tinking dis Sunday. Is dat too soon?"

"Is there any reason for such haste?" Jacob asked.

"I vas hoping to leaf Monday morning."

"Monday?" Margaret squeaked. Then, at normal volume, but rapidly, she went on in her complaint. "How are we supposed to arrange a wedding?"

"Remember, Mother?" Hannah interrupted. "No big wedding, no reception. There's nothing to arrange but to speak to Reverend Gunther."

"But Hannah! A girl only gets one wedding! We could get enough lace to make a dress, and you could get Clara Pederson and Jenny Smith to be bridesmaids."

Over the expanse of table, her eyes met Erik's. Her mouth quirked in an almost-smile. With a flash of teeth, he

23

winked at her. Her eyes skittered away. If she was to think straight, she had to look away, to try to keep her heart from fluttering in her throat.

"And Elizabeth," Margaret continued, "with Charity for a flower girl!"

"As you say, Mama, a girl only gets one wedding. I want mine to be just a few extra minutes in the church service.

"And Sunday sounds fine, now that I think about it. You all know I don't want this in the headlines. You also know that it wouldn't keep long in a small town, so the sooner the better."

"And you're leaving on Monday?" Jacob repeated, looking in disbelief at his daughter.

Erik answered. "If possible."

Jacob's next question was directed to him. "What are your plans? Where are you going? What are you going to do?"

Mr. Nelsson's eyes lit, burning with an excited glow. "Vest. To farm. I know dat dussn't sound trilling, but dis grass is amazing. I haf spent my vinter talking to men who haf been vest of here. Dey all say dat da grass goes on and on for miles. Vest of da Red River, but east of da vun hundret meridian. Land unsettled, yust vaiting to be claimed!

"Haf you seen dat grass?" He directed this at Jacob, then turned his enthusiasm back to include them all. "In some places it is tree feet tall! Soil dat grows grass like dat vould grow veat, oats, barley! And no vun is dere! Ve vould haf our choice. And no trees to cut out uff da vay first."

He pulled a paper from his shirt pocket and unfolded what turned out to be a hand-drawn map of North Dakota Territory. Large portions were blank, but the Missouri curved a wide arc in the southwest corner. The Red formed the eastern border, with the Sheyenne dumping into it. The James River formed a curvy line through the

24

southeast section and disappeared into South Dakota. The one hundredth meridian was penciled in its approximate location, as well as the towns of Bismarck and Mandan on the Missouri, and Grand Forks, further down the Red. There was, Erik said, a trading post at Pembina, in the northeast corner, and Fargo was marked as well.

He explained about the one hundredth meridian being a sort of demarcation line between land fit to ranch and land fit to farm. The land east of that line got more rain, and the grasses testified to the result.

His finger rested on an area northeast of Bismarck. "If ve settle near da beginning uff da Yames, ve vould have vater. But it is far to get vood for building. It is here and here." He indicated two spots, both in the extreme north of the territory. "Either place is vun hundret miles. And it is fifty or sixty miles to da claims office in Bismarck."

"Are you going alone?" Jacob asked.

"My friend, Halvor Yohannson, vill also go, and his vife."

"What about Indians?" Margaret wanted to know.

"Dey are dere," he answered without elaboration.

"I've had an offer for the store," Jacob said. All eyes turned to him. "Hannah knows nothing of this, but Maggie and I have spoken of joining you. We didn't know the specifics of where you were going, but we knew you were planning on homesteading. We've talked it over, and she's agreeable. What would you think of our coming along?"

Erik's grin was their answer. "Da more, da better!"

Hannah bit her lip to hold back the sudden tears. She'd been prepared to leave them, but she didn't need to! They were coming!

"It would be mighty hard for us to see Hannah go. Besides, this town is getting too civilized. But we don't have long. What needs doing?"

The afternoon went quickly.

Charity took a nap on Hannah's bed, then played with

some pots and pans on the floor by the table. Elizabeth and John kept themselves busy with a selection of books from the Campbells' shelves. They stayed in the parlor reading for hours, while the adults planned, made check-lists, and drank coffee.

Hannah was amazed at the magnitude of it. This was not a matter of hitching up a wagon and driving to where they built a house and threw some seeds into the ground. They needed seeds, yes, both grain and garden, but they also needed a plow and other tools, food, clothing, household goods, some furniture, and ammunition for their guns.

There were teams, two large horses for each wagon. The horses would pull plows when the time came. They were taking some milk cows, a few sheep for the wool, chickens for eggs, a couple of pigs and, to Hannah's surprise, dogs and cats. Each household would need one large dog to bark at the approach of visitors who might not be the welcome kind, as well as to protect the barn from wolves, coyotes, and foxes. The cats were to be for both the barns and houses, to keep away mice.

There would be rivers to cross, wagon wheels might need replacing, and there were medical supplies to consider. Erik Nelsson proved to be a storehouse of information. He'd spent most of the winter talking to men who had been through the area, and other places, drawing out their knowledge of land, weather, flora, fauna, Indians, and other hazards. He had borrowed a copy of *The Prairie Traveler* and read all of the pertinent parts. He knew how to make pemmican, how to get the wagons across the rivers, even how to treat snakebite. That, he said, was knowledge they wouldn't be needing. There were no poisonous snakes where they were going.

When the stretched rectangle of sunlight on the floor began fading, Hannah helped her mother bring in roast beef sandwiches and the rest of the cake. Margaret went to call the children to eat. Hannah set a plate in front of Erik, who seemed abashed to discover how long they had stayed.

"Tell me," she said, trying to make him feel natural and welcome to eat with them again, "about the housing arrangements you are planning." She sat once again across the table from him, giving him her attention. It wasn't just politeness. She wanted to know.

"But after we say a blessing," Jacob interrupted.

Soon they were discussing the wooded hills north of their destination, where they could go to get logs. They would need to travel to Bismarck for lumber. They talked about building design and necessary materials, and checked their lists to be sure they would have the needed tools. Charity fell asleep on Hannah's lap, sucking her thumb.

By the time they left, the older children were tired and cranky, but Jacob knew exactly what to do in the next four days, besides Sunday, that were left.

* * *

Hannah sat in front of her mirror in her camisole, brushing her hair. Her reflection frowned at her. If only she were pretty!

The eyes that stared at her so closely were a boring gray, not a warm brown or a striking blue or green. The chin was too square. Her hair was long, but not thick or curly. Her eyelashes were long and dark—the one feature she liked. Her nose was turned up on the end, with a scattering of freckles. Adorable on a schoolboy, but not on a grown woman. Her mouth was a disaster. Too wide. Teeth too big, bottom lip too full.

She made a face at herself.

Erik's smile and wink at the suggestion of Jenny Smith being her bridesmaid returned, in her memory as real as if he sat there in the mirror, and she muffled a giggle. He had a sense of humor. He was polite and well-mannered. He was intelligent. He was so handsome! She closed her eyes to savor the memory. Scorching, August-sky eyes. Hair like wheat, curling over his ears, but not tight curls. Straight nose, strong jaw, wide shoulders, long legs.

Could she really be considering marrying him? With a shudder, she blew out the candle and climbed into bed. More than considering. She'd given her word. All afternoon they'd made plans that revolved around her promise. But how could she ever make him happy?

* * *

She didn't see him again until Saturday evening. They had been busy selling the store, packing, cleaning, and gathering together all the items on the checklists. She assumed the Nelssons and the as yet unmet Johannsons were doing the same.

The new owner had taken over the store, but had graciously allowed them to stay in the rooms behind until Monday.

Rumors had been flying. Everyone in town knew that the three families were leaving, but as far as Hannah knew, tomorrow's wedding remained a secret.

In fact, she was sure on that point. Clara Pederson had come to visit a few hours ago, just before supper. She was excited for Hannah at the prospect of adventure, and also because she would be the only unmarried female in the vicinity of Erik Nelsson. If that wasn't an opportunity, what was? She was green with envy. "Why," she'd lamented, "couldn't *my* papa have a go at farming?"

Hannah smiled, remembering, when she rounded the corner to go from the kitchen to the parlor. Her father was just coming from the other direction. "Hello, Papa!" she greeted him.

"Is there any coffee made?"

He'd passed her by, and she turned to say "Yes, I just made a pot. Papa?"

"What?"

"Will there be room for my furniture?" It was a subject they'd discussed before. The answer had been, "We'll see, after we get all the important things." She knew that they couldn't possibly take everything, but she was hoping to have a few comforts. She thought he might have a clearer idea now.

"Your furniture is your furniture—as of tomorrow, Nelsson's furniture," he said with a grin. "Why don't you ask him?" He was finding this much more amusing than Hannah deemed necessary.

Sure. She would traipse through town, searching for Erik, asking his whereabouts and arousing curiosity, then look up into those unbelievable eyes and say, "Can we take my bed? My armoire? My basin and ewer and washstand? My vanity?"

She turned, not wanting to continue this talk when Jacob plainly was enjoying teasing her, and almost walked into Erik. He'd been standing so close behind her that she should have been able to feel him breathing! He'd heard everything. Thank goodness she hadn't verbalized her last thought!

His eyes were laughing at the little joke on her, but not maliciously.

Standing this close, she could see the sapphire ring around his turquoise irises. His skin was flawless. He had lines at the corners of his eyes and the sides of his mouth. He was perfect. There was no other word.

"So vy don't you ask me?" he carried on the game. Perfect teeth. Not even bad breath.

For a second, she'd been staring, mesmerized, but his question brought a flood of modesty with a blush to match. She dropped her gaze, and he took pity on her. "How much furniture do you haf?"

"Just the things in my room," she answered plainly,

refusing to let her embarrassment get the better of her. "I'll show you." She stepped past him, and he followed her, revealing another person who'd been standing behind him. Hannah had seen the man around town, but she had never been introduced to him.

"Oh," Erik said. "I forget my manners again. Dis is my good friend Halvor Yohannson. He and his vife go vit us. His English is no good." He went on to introduce her, in Norwegian. The only word she understood was her own name.

He was slightly shorter than Erik and about ten or fifteen years older. His blond hair was thinning and had a reddish cast.

"Pleased to meet you." She bobbed a brief curtsy, then led the way back across the parlor to open one of the two doors.

Her room was her private world, and she was pleased with it. There was a real brass bed with a real mattress. The other furniture was French, cherry wood. The roses on her pitcher were hand painted. She'd made the curtains, quilt, dust ruffle, pillow shams, and rugs by herself. She knew the room was lovely.

There were two trunks, too. One held all her clothing, which she'd packed from the armoire. The other was her "hope chest." She'd filled it years ago, back when she'd hoped, with blankets and pillows and silverware and doilies—all the things needed to start a home. The trunks were going. If she had to buy a wagon and drive it herself, the trunks were going.

"All dis is important to you?"

She hated the idea of giving up any of it, but if she must, she must. "The two trunks have to come," she said. "If there is any room beyond that, I leave it to you to choose what to take."

Just then there was a knock on the door that opened

into the parlor from the store, and a bellowing voice called, "Campbell!"

Jacob opened the door. The new owner said, "There's a baby out here and a—oh, you better just come out and see!"

They all traipsed into the store, even Margaret, who'd come out from the kitchen at the loud knock.

Sure enough, there was a baby. A girl, about six or seven months old. She had the features and skin color of an Indian, but her hair was tobacco brown, and there was a liberal dusting of gold flecks in her light brown eyes.

An Indian woman with long, graying hair and many wrinkles held her lovingly. Mr. Bucher, the new owner of the store, had returned behind the counter, where an old, bearded trapper leaned on one elbow.

Joe Bucher opened his mouth, then shut it again before he finally spoke. "The store was closed, but I was still here working, and these folks were pretty insistent on coming in. They're looking for—" He turned to the trapper and said, "Why don't *you* tell them?"

"Name's Travis McGee," the man said, but made no move to shake hands. "I wuz jist 'splainin' 'bout this papoose. A girl come through Fort Union last September. She'd jist been rescued from the Piegans.

"She stayed jist long enough to leave this here papoose. Didn't never even wanna see it after she had it. Soon uz she could travel, she lit out east, fast as she could go. My squaw ere's been tendin' her. She don't want ta part with 'er, neither, but it jist ain't practical! We's on our way to Winnipeg ta see my kids an' then buy some s'pplies before headin' back to Montany." His eyes took on a sad, faraway look. "It jist ain't the same no more. Too many people." He refocused on the present.

"Anyways, we cain't haul a squallin' infant all the way ta Winnipeg, and we ain't found no one yet eager to take no

31

half-breed papoose ta raise. We're leavin' 'er here, even if it's on the church steps, but my woman'd take it better if it's with someone. An' I ain't hurtin' 'er feelin's none. She don't speak no English." He gestured toward the baby. "You know anybody who'd want her?"

Joe Bucher shrugged. "I don't know folks in town yet, and I surely wouldn't know what to do with a baby. Thought you might have a suggestion."

"I might," Jacob started, but Erik didn't let him finish.

"Ve vill take her." He walked to the woman and reached for the baby.

At a command from the old trapper, she handed the child to Erik. The woman's black eyes were shiny wet as she turned and walked out of the store.

Hannah's heart went out to her.

"Dat is, I mean . . . Hannah?" Erik, holding the baby in the crook of his arm, looked to Hannah.

"Church steps, indeed!" Hannah took the few steps required to stand by Erik. The baby stopped trying to discover what wonderful, lumpy thing was in his shirt pocket and reached instead for the pink ribbon bow at the neck of Hannah's dress. Hannah gave her an enamelled tin salt shaker from the shelf. It had a lid, and later she could put in a few dry beans to make a nice noisy toy. Her reward was a fat-cheeked, drooling grin which revealed four teeth, two on top and two on the bottom.

"I'll pay you for that later this evening," she said to Mr. Bucher.

"No, no," said Jacob, getting out his change purse. "My gift to my latest grandchild!"

"Are you sure?" Erik asked her. "Are four new children all at once too much?"

"I love children. And Lisa and John are big enough to help."

"Lisa?" He frowned.

32

Hannah colored, discovered in the liberty she had been taking mentally since the day she met the children. "You say 'Eleesabett.' " She gave a fair imitation of his accent. "So I always think of her as 'Lisa.' But I will try to remember to call her Elizabeth if you don't like it."

Erik chuckled. "Lisa is good. I tink I like it." He turned to the old trapper. "Vat is da baby's name?"

"Ruth." The man went to the door. "Glad to've found her a home. Evenin.' " He closed the door behind him.

Erik let Ruth bang his chest with her shalt shaker. "Root." He smiled down at her.

To the astonishment of everyone present, Hannah abruptly took the baby from Erik and handed her to Margaret, then took Erik by the hand and led him outside. She turned left and started up the hill to the bluff overlooking the river.

"Vere are ve going?"

"I need to show you something." He'd made no move to take his hand from hers, but now she let him go, thinking she was too forward.

Soon they were on the bluff, near the trees under which he had proposed. There was a large, gnarled root on the ground. Hannah should know; she'd tripped over it twice.

"This," she said, kicking it, "is a *root*. I mean no offense, and you can pronounce any other word however you wish, but you simply cannot call a little girl 'Root.' "

There was silence. She had no indication how he was taking her presumptuous, unsolicited English lesson. "I hope you don't think me rude?"

"No." He leaned an arm over his head on a low branch. "You vill haf to teach me da right vay to say her name, den."

"Is there enough light? Can you see my mouth?"

"I see you kvite vell in da moonlight."

Yes, she imagined he could. The half moon was behind

33

him, leaving his face in heavy shadow but shining on his blond hair like a halo. Facing him, she was in the direct light.

"Put your tongue under your front teeth, like this." She showed him. "Then pull it back, quickly. Th. Th."

He tried it and got a "th" sound.

"Good!" She smiled. "Now try Ruth." She said it a few times, stressing the "th," which he managed to copy.

"That's wonderful! Now she is Ruth, instead of Root. There is another 'th' sound, so you don't get confused. It's harder, like in this or these. Try it."

"Hannah." He reached for her hand and pulled her a step closer. Her face was already tilted up, questioning him silently in complete innocence, so his kiss was unexpected. And brief. By the time she realized his intention it was over, and the aftermath was just beginning. Everything inside her was limp and useless. She was surprised. Stunned was more accurate. She took a few seconds to regain confidence in her legs, then whispered, "Why did you do that?"

"Becoss I vanted to. And vile I haf you out here, I vant to say tank . . . thank you."

"What for?"

"For being villing to giff up so much for me. You vould leaf your mama and papa, and you vould leaf your beautiful furniture and comfortable home. That tells me you trust me vit your future. I only hope I can liff up to it."

There were so many things she wanted to say, but her feelings were so new and strong. She didn't know how to express them. For that matter, did she want to? It was much too soon for any declarations.

"Come." This time he led her. He'd never let go of her hand since he'd pulled her toward him. Still he held it, naturally, as they walked back.

He released it to open the store's door for her. "Vun

more thing." He stopped with his hand on the door. "I'm glad you asked for time to think before you said yes. If you had said yes right away, I vould haf vondered about your motives, and I vould be looking for a vay to back out." The outer door swung open, then the door to the parlor. She was relieved that he'd released her hand. It was bad enough that they'd run off together, without returning holding hands.

Her father and Erik's friend Halvor were intent on the hand-drawn map. Margaret sat with them at the table, crocheting a doily. All three faces turned at their entrance, faces too polite to ask questions.

"English lessons," Hannah said abruptly, and reached for two more mugs.

"And vere is Ruth?" Erik asked, very carefully pronouncing the name.

Margaret's grin lit her face. "She is sleeping on my bed. What a darling! Of course, I had to fold some towels—we haven't had any diapers around here for years! But I made up a bottle, and she's sound asleep."

Hannah set a cup of coffee in front of Erik, who was sitting in back of the table near Halvor.

"Thank you."

"You're welcome." She sat between her parents.

"Thank goodness you're back," Jacob said to Erik. "Communication here is not the best."

That started them on a long discussion while Margaret crocheted and Hannah kept the cups filled.

Chapter 3

Early, when the sky was a pearly gray, Hannah woke up and got on her knees by her bed. Thanking God for the day, asking for the strength of will to do His will was easy enough, but she couldn't put into words her request for His blessing on this important day. She hoped the prayer of her heart was good enough.

She took a bath and put on her new dress. It was a pale, misty gray with an ivory lace collar. There was shell pink piping around the collar and cuffs, the buttons down the front were pink, and there was a pink cloth rose on the neck front. She'd made it at her mother's insistence for an upcoming dance and had never worn it. The gray made her eyes look bigger. For once she was glad she'd listened to her mother and her "this will look pretty on you" nonsense, though at the time she had only acquiesced to humor her.

But what to do with her hair! Her usual braid down the back wouldn't do.

"Mama?" she called out of her room.

"In here." Hannah followed the voice to the kitchen, where she found Margaret feeding Ruth. The baby sat up and grinned, but refused to eat any more of the pasty concoction on the spoon.

"Good morning, sweetheart!" Hannah wet a rag and wiped Ruth's face, then picked her up for a cuddle. "Is Grandma making you eat that? Would you prefer to have a cracker?" The dimpled brown fingers wrapped around the cracker, but she didn't eat it. She was too busy poking at Hannah's eyes and mouth, exploring.

"That's a sight I've waited a long time for, Hannah. You're a natural mother. I hope you have twelve."

"Twelve total, or twelve more?"

"Well," Margaret said with a laugh, "I admit that the way you've collected children lately, you could have twelve by next week."

Hannah rolled her eyes. "I think four are enough!"

"I trust you mean for now? But never mind that. What was it you wanted?"

"My hair. Could you help me do something with it?"

A bleary-eyed Jacob came into the kitchen and poured himself a cup of coffee. "Just the man I wanted to see!" Margaret handed him the baby, along with a bottle.

She braided Hannah's hair, but from the top of her head, and loosely, then pinned it up. She pulled a few strands loose at her neck and went to fetch her curling iron, which she set on the stove to heat.

"Eat," she instructed.

"I couldn't possibly."

Margaret took a scissor and cut a foot off the hair she'd pulled loose. "A few escaped tendrils is charming, but we can't have them hanging to your waist."

The loose hair curled quickly, and Margaret stood back to inspect her work. "Hannah, you're beautiful!"

Hannah hurried to her room to be alone with her mirror and her reaction.

She didn't look like herself. The looseness of the braid let her hair billow a bit around her face. The two strands at the neck were hardly curled at all, looking indeed escaped and making the style less severe. She looked softer. She liked it. Would Erik?

* * *

Hannah sat between her mother and father, holding Ruth.

From time to time she had dressed especially nice for church, so she didn't think anyone would make anything of it. Besides, they were distracted by Ruth. Where had she come from? Why had they taken her? She was hard pressed to leave Erik out of the story.

When the Nelsson family walked into the church, Hannah stared resolutely ahead, but she could see them from the corner of her eye. The children were clean and groomed. Except for John's pants being too short and Charity almost bursting the seams of her dress, they appeared well cared for in every way. Erik was wearing a black suit and tie with a white shirt.

She felt panicky. There was less than an hour left for her to change her mind. Was she doing the right thing?

Closing her eyes, she concentrated. She believed it was right. She'd prayed, she read her Bible, she'd asked her father, and she'd followed what she felt God saying to her. She'd also asked herself, honestly, if it was because Erik was so handsome that she had consented. No. He loved his children. He was fun, he was funny. He was smart. Mostly, he loved God. *Handsome,* she thought, smiling inwardly, *is just icing on the cake.*

But for him, there was no icing. And she wasn't even

39

sure how he felt about the Hannah that was inside. He was only solving a problem.

How can I do this? her heart cried.

Sitting in church, the last minutes ticking away, the cry echoed desperately within her. Her fear grew. Not just the fear of rejection, fear that he would regret this, but fear of him. What did she know of him, really? But her parents were coming along. How bad could a man be who welcomed his bride's parents to live alongside him? The word "bad" just didn't fit Erik. "Bad" men didn't enjoy babies banging their chests with tin cups.

One of her favorite psalms came to mind. "The Lord is my strength and my shield; my heart trusted in him and I am helped: therefore my heart greatly rejoiceth; and with my song will I praise Him."

Margaret nudged her with her elbow, taking the baby and giving her a conspiratorial grin.

"I've cut my sermon short this morning," the pastor was saying.

The service was over, and Hannah hadn't heard a word of it!

". . . because I have on this occasion the privilege of performing one of my most joyful duties."

Hannah heard the sudden, expectant stillness.

"Two of our little family of God wish to commit themselves to each other in the bonds of holy matrimony."

An excited buzz filled the church.

"Would Mr. Erik Nelsson—"

Another hush.

"—and Miss Hannah Campbell please come forward?"

A gasp, followed by a louder buzz.

Hannah rose to her feet and stepped past her mother. Her hands were so shaky that she clutched her skirt to still them. Her knees were wobbly, and she thought she would faint.

Erik had been seated toward the front and was already standing by Reverend Gunther. His tanned face contrasted with the white of his shirt. Her own face felt as white as a sheet. She must look like a ghost compared to him.

How could she get her legs to function sufficiently to carry her to the front? "The Lord is my strength and my shield," she whispered. She took a calming breath and started forward.

The marriage ceremony went quickly.

"I do."

"I do."

"By the authority . . . I now pronounce . . ."

Gold band on cold finger.

"You may kiss the bride."

It wasn't love shining in her eyes. It was terror. He wasn't kissing her so much as he was helping her remain standing.

Then she was seated in the pew next to Lisa. Charity climbed onto her lap. Erik took a few seconds to collect Ruth from Margaret before sitting between Hannah and John.

He leaned over to whisper in her ear. "Are you feeling vell?"

She nodded.

"Are you sure then, Mrs. Nelsson, that this is vat you vant? Ve could refuse to sign the papers. But it vould be a vaste uff a pritty dress."

Hannah pressed her forehead to Charity's hair, hoping to hide her pink face. Mrs. Nelsson. Pretty dress. Good heavens!

After the Doxology, they stood by the pastor at the door to receive congratulations. Hannah was between Erik and Reverend Gunther. Ruth was with the Campbells, and the other three children went outside.

Well-wishers and those who pretended to be well-wishers passed by, shaking hands. "Congratulations!" "Good

41

luck!" "I'm so happy for you!" Some walked on, speaking to each other in low tones. Hannah saw the range of emotions she'd expected. Mostly surprise, mixed with a degree of dismay that he'd married so poorly. But that was on the faces of only a few, all of them women. Hannah held up her chin and forced a smile to her lips.

Clara Pederson was last in the line. Her red-blond hair was curled beautifully, hanging down her back and over one shoulder in ringlets and she wore a new dress. It seemed to Hannah that she was rather abrupt in congratulating Erik.

When she came to Hannah, she gave her hand a short jerk that passed for a handshake and glared at her through misted eyes. "You might have told me," she sputtered through tightly clenched teeth.

Hannah felt sorry for her. If asked to predict the next Mrs. Nelsson, anyone in town would've said Clara, including Hannah and, obviously, including Clara. Perhaps she should have told her ahead of time. But telling Clara was like taking out an advertisement in the newspaper. She'd get over it.

A group of men was passing through town on their way to work on the railroad somewhere west of Bismarck. Hannah was surprised to see such a group in church, but they were there. Clara had noticed them, too, and as Hannah watched, her friend's dropped handkerchief was rapidly retrieved by a good-looking lad of about seventeen. Clara thanked him with a demure smile.

Erik, who was also watching the scene, gave a snort of humor. "Heartbroken, isn't she?"

Hannah glanced up at him. He was more astute than she'd given him credit for. She turned to watch the red-gold curls bounce the rest of the way down the steps, and noticed the extra sway in Clara's walk as she passed the men.

Out on the grass, she could also see her mother. She was

talking to some women and wearing a broad, happy smile. Her plump hands were in perpetual motion. She, if no one else, was ecstatic with the day's event.

She felt the gentle pressure of Erik's hand at the back of her waist and looked up from her thoughts. Reverend Gunther had produced the marriage license. With a twinkle in his eye, Erik offered her the pen.

In a way, he was proposing again. Her smile was frightened, wavering, but she took the pen.

Descending the church steps, his hand slipped around her waist again. The children fell in line behind them. Hannah felt as though everyone was gawking at her, with her undeserved husband and the children following behind like a family of ducks.

"I have a huge roast in the oven," Margaret said to Erik. "You are all welcome to join us for dinner."

"Thank you. That vould be nice, and ve vill yoin you in a few minutes. Vould you mind very much to take all the children to your house vith you? Ve vill be soon."

Margaret, in deprived-grandma heaven, agreed.

"And ask your friends over," she called over her shoulder. "I'd like to get to know them before we are trailmates."

"Ya, I vill ask them."

He took Hannah's hand and started walking. Almost as soon as they started, she knew they were headed to the tree above the river.

Though only for a short time, it was "their" place. She stood, watching the activity on the water, enjoying the breeze, the flowers, the grass.

Erik took off his suit coat and spread it on the grass. "I don't vant you to get your dress dirty."

He got on his knees on the coat, and held his hand out to her. When she knelt, facing him, he took her other hand, too. "I vant to start this marriage right," he said.

He prayed for wisdom, for provision, for them each to

43

always treat the other with kindness, for protection, for health, for the children's spiritual welfare. All the vague thoughts she'd had earlier that morning, he put into words before God. Any lingering apprehensions Hannah may have had were erased.

Too soon, he was getting to his feet and helping her up. He bent to retrieve his coat, and hooked it over his shoulder.

The springtime sunlight was muted by the budding leaves of the tree that dappled Hannah's upturned face with shadow. "Thank you for doing that. I'll always treasure the memory."

"Now, in my eyes, ve are married."

After a leading statement like that, she half expected him to kiss her. There was an unfamiliar look on his face that she thought might mean he wanted to, but he only started walking back down the hill.

Well, what did she know?

He didn't even take her hand. She was totally baffled.

They had walked almost back into town, side by side, but like two strangers. Was this the same man who had held her hand in the moonlight? She asked a question to break the silence between them.

"So will I finally get to meet the mysterious Hilda Johannson?"

"Vy do you say mysterious?"

"Because I'm beginning to wonder if there really is such a person."

His smile lit her day. Who cared if he didn't feel like holding her hand?

"You didn't tink . . . think I leave the children alone ven ve are talking so much to your papa?"

"She doesn't mind?"

"She thinks she is their mother."

That gave her pause. "Then why was it so important for you to get married?"

"She does not liff in my house. She helps ven I need somevun to vatch them. She has even cooked for us. But she is not there to help vith putting them to bed or giving them a bath. Lisa does that for Charity. Then there is the laundry and the sewing. Hilda has her own house to run."

"I see." He'd solved his problem in the only logical, practical, thoroughly unromantic way available.

He knocked on the door of a small house, opened by a tall, large-boned woman with brown hair that she wore in braids twisted over the top of her head like a crown. Between her front teeth was a gap which always showed because she was always smiling. Hannah had seen her around town, as she had Halvor, but not as often.

"Come in, come in!" The big woman stood back and held the door wide.

"Hilda Yohannson." Erik began the introduction as he stepped in behind Hannah. "This is Hannah Nelsson."

It was the first time Hannah had heard her new name spoken like that. Hannah Nelsson. She liked it.

Imagine! This man, so wonderful in every way she'd discovered so far, had actually married her! Though she had heard "Hannah Nelsson" from his own lips, though she wore his ring, it wasn't quite believable. Hannah Nelsson.

"So this is the Hannah I've heard so much about!" Hilda extended her hand for a shake.

Hannah's ears had been prepared to hear another heavy Norwegian accent, and she was startled to hear Hilda's eastern speech.

"Pleased to meet you, Mrs. Johansson. I've heard a good deal about you, too. But are you not Norwegian?"

"Ya, shoe-er." She mimicked the accent with outrageous exaggeration, wearing a wicked grin. "My parents were from Norway," she continued. "My father was a whaler. They moved to Boston, and I was born and raised there. Sit down. I'll get some coffee."

45

"Ve can't. My new mother-in-law is expecting us for dinner. She vants you to come, too. And you haf to meet our new daughter, Ruth."

"Ah, Ruth, is it? Not Root?"

Erik chuckled. "My vife, it seems, has some strong opinions about vat is a good name."

Hilda laughed and patted Hannah's shoulder. "I think I like you. Already you have him improving his English. After all these years, I can't get my Halvor even to try and speak it."

"Vere is he?"

"He is already at the Campbells'. He wanted to ask Jacob something about the other wagon."

"What other wagon?" asked Hannah.

"He must mean my vagon," Erik said. "There are still some kvestions about vat to pack vere."

"So, Mrs. Johannson—" Hannah said, as the three walked out the door and back toward town.

"Please call me Hilda. I am not a formal person. We will soon be traveling together, and in a rather primitive, uncomfortable means of conveyance, I might add. I can't imagine you saying, 'Please pass the sugar, Mrs. Johannson,' as though we were having tea in a Boston parlor."

"Then you must call me Hannah."

A few steps.

"You were saying, Hannah?"

"Oh yes. It strikes me as odd—well, forgive me if I'm being nosy, but why weren't you at the wedding?"

Hilda's warmth and friendliness vanished. "I am no friend of churches."

Hannah didn't know what to say. That explained why she had never met the Johannsons at church or at the town's few social occasions, which centered around the church. Maybe someday, when she knew Hilda better, she would pursue the topic.

Chapter 4

Hannah waited.

Erik had said something about giving her some privacy, and had gone out the back door.

At first she'd simply stood there.

Exploring his rented one-room house hadn't taken long. There were a stove, some cupboards, a table with two benches, a poorly made armoire, a washstand, and a bed. A second bed was curtained off in the corner. The furniture was sturdy, but ugly and scratched.

As far as she could guess, the girls had shared one bed, and John had been sleeping with his father. It was a good thing they were moving on. Where would Erik have put the two extra family members he had recently acquired?

Hannah sat, nervous and growing more so, on the edge of the bed, brushing her hair. She was in her nightgown. She'd washed. How much time did he think she needed? It must already be after ten.

She had to smile, remembering how Hilda and her mother had argued politely over who would keep the children. Erik had warned them that traveling and then living so close, they would soon tire of the patter of little feet. His comment had drawn a frown on Lisa's face.

"Maybe so," Margaret had said, "but I'm not tired yet. Let them stay here."

In the end Lisa, John, and Charity had gone home with Hilda, since they knew her better. For the same reason, Margaret kept Ruth.

Hannah's hair crackled and popped from all the brushing. Her nerves were on the verge of snapping, too. Where was he? She set down the brush and went to look.

When she opened the door, his low, quiet voice spoke in the darkness. "Come here."

"In my nightgown?!" Her whisper was scandalized. She heard him laughing softly.

"It is dark. There is no vun around. Come look at these lights! Isn't God amazing?"

Her eyes were drawn to the pulsing green and yellow glow in the sky above the buildings to the north. Barefoot, she went out and stood by him to watch.

Erik drew her back to his chest and put an arm around her waist.

"Yes," she murmured. "God is quite amazing."

"I haf not seen those lights since before I left home. They are beautiful."

The April night was chilly, and Hannah shivered. Erik put his other arm around her, too.

"Hannah, vy did you marry me?"

It wasn't a question she was expecting. The bald truth, she decided, was her best answer. The truth her father had helped her see.

"Because my other option at this point was to grow old

alone, and eventually have to go to live with my uncle or one of his sons and have an exciting and meaningful life full of needlework in his parlor. In case you didn't notice, there wasn't a line of men beating down my father's door for me." Better to state the fact openly than have him think it in secret. "Your children are more important than embroidering pillowcases."

His arms tightened.

"Vat about the two men in Visconsin who vanted to marry you?"

"How did you know about that?"

"Yacob told me."

Bless him. He wouldn't have Erik believing his daughter was totally desperate for a husband.

"I admit a large part of my reason for refusing Mr. Taylor was because he was shorter than I am. But he was also very much older, and I didn't want to be a young widow."

"You could be anyvay."

"Taking that chance and writing out a guarantee are two different things."

She could feel him moving in a noiseless laugh. His shoulder was behind her head, and she rested back against him.

"The other," she went on, "was a drunk."

"So you agree to marry me becoss I fit your kvalifications? Vun of vich is that I am tall enough?"

Hannah blushed in the darkness. She had thought it unromantic of him to marry her because she fit his list of "must be" and "must not be." Yet she'd done the same thing. Talk about having a log in one's own eye! The cold bite of shame worried her heart.

"I suppose so," she admitted.

"If I vere to ask you again, now that you know me better, vould you say yes yust becoss it vas *me* asking? Do you like me?"

49

"Yes, I like you, and I'm afraid I would say yes."

"Vy do you say it like that?"

"Because it wouldn't be very smart."

"Then I, too, am not smart." He turned her in his arms. "I like you very much." This kiss was not so brief.

* * *

Hannah knew where she was immediately when the crack of light under the blind woke her. There was no sense of unfamiliarity with her surroundings. The warmth of Erik's chest behind her, the weight of his arm draped across her waist. . . . His even breathing, gently on the back of her neck, led her to believe he was sleeping.

She could get used to waking up like this. There was never a time in her life when she remembered feeling so safe and warm.

But there was much to do today, and quickly! They had to finish packing and loading and be on their way. What about breakfast? She knew there was no food in this house to cook. What did he expect of her?

Carefully, slowly, she pulled back the covers and started to ease her way from under his arm. He pulled her back. "Vere are you going?"

"Breakfast?" Her voice sounded to herself like a scared mouse.

"Ve are going to your Mama's for breakfast."

"We are?"

"You vere sitting right there ven ve talked about it."

"I was?"

"Ya. Don't you remember? The night of my English lessons?"

No, she didn't remember. "Are you sure?"

He raised up on an elbow and looked down at her with a sleepy, lopsided smile. "Ya, I am sure."

The vivid color of his eyes shocked her anew. The night's

50

growth of beard was like sprinkled gold dust on sculpt-
ed marble.

This had to be a dream. She reached out her hand to
explore the texture of his cheek. After a moment he
clasped her hand and brought it to his mouth for a lingering kiss on her palm.

"What time is breakfast?" she whispered, remembering
what they were talking about.

"Ten-thirty."

"Why so late?"

"I don't know. Maybe, Hannah, your mother vas once a
bride?"

* * *

Hannah lay on her stomach, watching him shave. Except
for shoes and socks, and braiding her hair, she was ready
to face the day. She propped her chin on her fist.

Erik glanced at her sideways. His smile was less daz-
zlingly white surrounded by shaving cream, but no less
effective. "Vat are you doing?"

"Absolutely nothing. And enjoying it!"

He pulled out a pocket watch and casually flipped it open.
"It is ten-fifteen. Perhaps you should be doing something."

"Oh, my goodness!" She scrambled for her stockings. It
was hard to lace her shoes. Her hair got in the way. She
should've braided it first.

Erik had finished shaving and was peering out of the still
closed blind. As soon as she fastened the end of her hair he
reached for her hand, wearing a sly, smug look.

"What is going on?"

"Nothing more than vas planned."

"What plan?" Suspicion narrowed one eye, and she tilted
her head slightly to one side.

"Come." He tugged on the hand he held. "I show you."

Outside stood a different wagon, pulled by a strange
team. The wagon was loaded with her furniture—all of it.

51

All the Campbells, Nelssons, and Johannsons stood in the street awaiting her reaction.

Hannah put her hands to her face. She wanted to cry. It was so sweet, and so totally unexpected.

"How—" she started to ask, but her voice broke and she couldn't finish the question.

"Easy. I bought another vagon and team. Hilda vill drife it. It is your vedding present."

"Thank you!" She threw her arms around his neck.

"Not here," Erik said, pulling her arms down.

Hannah didn't stop to think about it. "You do so much for me!" she rushed on. "Ruth, and my parents coming, and now this! Thank you!" It was difficult to keep from hugging him in her excitement, but he turned from her to where his friends and family stood by the wagon only a few feet away. "There is too much to do for us to be standing around. Let's eat and get the vagons loaded."

A terrible understanding suddenly crushed her. He was ashamed of her. He liked her, she didn't doubt that, but he'd married her out of obedience and necessity. She was realistic enough to figure that she ranked somewhere below Halvor on his list of friends, but he didn't want to flaunt her in front of the world.

Unfortunately, her feelings for him were nothing of this kind. She'd only known him a week, but already she thought of him as the best friend she'd ever had. He was real, not pretending anything. She knew she could tell him anything and he would not mock or belittle her or betray her confidence. Yes, it was her misfortune to have fallen in love with the man.

Stepping to the wagon, she ran a hand over the smooth, curving leg of her washstand. She made no attempt to stop her tears.

"Hannah?" Margaret put a hand on her shoulder. "Are you all right, honey?"

Hannah smiled. It wasn't hard. She knew Eric honestly

52

did like her. He would never hurt her intentionally. And it wasn't as though he could change his feelings just because he wanted to. She would love him anyway. It wasn't possible for her to do any less.

"Isn't this wonderful, Mama?" She stroked the smooth finish again. "He's so thoughtful. It's all a little overwhelming."

"I'm so happy for you!" Margaret hugged her tight.

* * *

Jacob and Margaret's wagon was first, loaded with trunks, food, tools, and some of their furniture. Most of that had been too large and impractical to take along, like the dining room table and the horsehair sofa. A cage of chickens was tied to the rear.

Hilda drove the next wagon, the one that carried Hannah's furniture and all the extra odds and ends from all three families. It also had all the canvas and poles they would use to make tents when they first got to wherever they were going. It would take awhile to get logs and lumber and build cabins.

Next would be John and Erik, walking, to keep the cows, sheep, and pigs headed in the right direction. With any luck, two of the dogs would help in that endeavor.

The third dog they'd found was too young to walk so far. The Nelsson children had immediately claimed and dubbed the puppy Passop, which made Erik and Halvor laugh. Hilda explained that while the name meant "lookout," it was the Norwegian equivalent of Fido. Passop would walk sometimes and ride other times in the next wagon, which Hannah drove.

She referred to this wagon fondly as the "circus wagon," because in addition to Passop, the wagon carried the three girls and a basket containing a yellow-eyed white cat and six multicolored kittens.

Halvor, in his own wagon, brought up the rear. That was for defense.

Erik lifted Lisa up through the opening in the canvas at the back of the wagon, earning an exasperated "Papa!" She was quite capable of climbing up without his help. Next he tossed in Charity, who landed with a bounce and a delighted squeal on the pile of blankets and pillows arranged for their comfort. He set Ruth beside her, and the baby began exploring right away. There were too many drawers and trunks to try to open, and too many boxes and bags to empty.

He met Hannah's smile with one of his own. "Thank you," he said, "for letting me keep her." He was half joking, making her sound like a stray pup, but he was quite serious, too.

Together they walked up the side of the wagon to the front. "I wanted to thank you, too," she said, "for making it possible to take all my things. I didn't expect it. I thought you were poor."

His expression went sober. "Vy did you think that?"

"I never thought about it beyond what Papa said."

"Vich vas?"

"When I asked him if I should marry you, he said you probably weren't rich, or you wouldn't be out here. Your house, or the one you rented, confirmed the idea."

"That house vas a shack. It vas also the only shack available to rent." They came to a stop near the seat. "You vere villing to marry me, thinking I vas poor?"

"Most people are poor. I didn't think about it one way or the other."

"Hannah, I am not rich, so it is a good thing you didn't think I vas." He searched her face. "You should know how ve stand.

"A homestead claim is vun hundred and sixty acres. The gufferment vill sell it for vun dollar and twenty-fife cents an acre. I do not haf two hundret dollars. Ve haff to stay there the full fife years before it is ours. And I think, to start vith, the farm vill take ef'ry penny I haf."

"Why do you sound apologetic? We will have food. You're going to build a real house, and, thanks to you, we will have some real furniture to put in it. I couldn't ask for more."

He helped her up to the seat and squeezed her hand before releasing it. Their eyes met and held for a long second, then he softly asked, "Are you ready?"

With a mute nod, she tore her eyes away. How could she possibly feel such a staggering emotion for someone she'd only known for eight days?

"Then let's go!" he said, with the jubilant grin of a child with a new pony.

This was it. They were leaving Fargo. Hannah's eyes traveled all around, with a sense she hadn't expected, that she would miss this place. Why, she didn't know, unless it was just because she had seen it grow from nothing. But it was just a small town on the edge of forever. There was nothing here, really, to miss.

The only friends she had here were the sort of friends one had because of geography. They had nothing in common, and if they'd been in a town of any size, they wouldn't have taken up with one another.

Take Clara, for example. If they had met in New York or Boston or even Minneapolis, Hannah would probably have considered her to be a floozy. Clara would have found Hannah dreadfully boring. But since geography forced frequent exposure, they learned to look beyond exteriors and find a mutual tolerance which grew to affection.

Hannah searched the crowd of townspeople who had turned out to see them leave, and found her friend. Wordlessly, they said their good-byes. In Clara's face she saw sorrow at their parting, envy for the excitement of it, and a touch of covetousness in the glance the green eyes flashed at Erik briefly.

The wheels turned. Hannah looked back and saw Clara

lift her hand in a wave. She responded, but Clara never saw it. A handsome man on a palomino was just dismounting in front of the saloon.

Hannah left Fargo with a laugh. Clara would be Clara.

* * *

Lisa sat at the back of the wagon stroking the cat. Hannah wished she would sit up by her so they could get to know each other, but she didn't suggest it. She knew the feeling of being forced to move away from friends to a virtually uninhabited area, but she had been an adult. It had to be worse for Lisa.

Ruth started crying, and Hannah had to stop to change her diapers. Erik waited impatiently. A few miles further, they were forced to stop again because both Charity and Ruth were getting fussy. They were hungry and tired of being confined.

"At this rate," Erik stormed, "it vill take us until August to get there!"

Wisely, Hannah let it pass. He was angry with circumstances, not her.

"They are tired and hungry. How long will we continue tonight?"

"A couple uff hours yet. Tomorrow ve vill need to make a different arrangement."

Hannah gave each of them a cracker and took up the reins.

"Ve are not stopping again. Eleesabett, you tend to those babies until then!"

They stopped when it was getting dark, but still light enough to make supper and feed and water the animals.

Halvor and Jacob unhitched the horses while Erik got a fire going. He hung a big kettle on a tripod over it, then said "Ladies," with a theatrical sweep of his hand. It was now their duty to make supper.

Hannah was tired. She hurt from all the bumping and

56

jolting on the hard board seat. Her patience was already sorely tried with children and animals and the bossy attitude of this apparent slave-driver she had married. Her scowl followed him.

She wanted to relax, soak her sore hands, and sleep. But there was supper to make, dishes to wash, children to tend to. Where was her pioneer spirit? Where was her stamina?

"The Lord is my strength," she said to herself.

Charity was glad to get out and run. Ruth she let crawl around, with Lisa to make sure she didn't eat dirt and grass or anything more offensive.

Margaret began to peel potatoes and Hilda to slice carrots as Hannah filled the large kettle with water. A shot made her jump, and she dropped the jar she was using. The grass kept the jar from breaking, but she splashed water all over the front of her skirt.

Indians? She saw nothing. A snake? No. He wouldn't be shooting a snake in an area where none were poisonous. She scanned the horizon in a circle, and seeing nothing, hearing nothing, she went back to her water hauling. Soon there was another shot.

The other two women also paused, curious and a little afraid, but Halvor and Jacob had finished picketing the horses and were back near the fire. They didn't seem concerned.

With a shrug, Hannah started a pot of coffee. Halvor went to milk the cows, and Jacob went with him to learn how.

"Gotta teach this old dog new tricks," he said, but he was happy enough to learn.

"I think only John is more exuberant about this adventure than Jacob." Margaret gave a tired smile. "Myself, I'm wondering. Have we lost our minds?"

"I think so," Hannah agreed without looking up.

Erik came and handed her two dead rabbits. "They vill

57

cook kvickly and ve von't haf to use our supplies." He walked off.

Hannah got a sharp knife and went away from the others to clean the rabbits. She wasn't sure she knew how. It wasn't something she'd done before.

A quick slash split the first rabbit open. It was worse than she'd anticipated. The muscles of her throat tightened, but, holding her breath, she pushed her hand into the cavity to pull out the insides.

The deep breath didn't work, and she was glad there was no one around to see her humiliate herself by being sick in the grass. She went on. Going to Erik and saying she could not do this would be worse. He would either laugh at her or get angry. Either one was not what she wanted to see on his face.

The second rabbit was a bit easier, and skinning them wasn't so bad. It took longer, but wasn't as gory. When they were done, she took them to the small creek that ran by their camp to wash and cut into smaller chunks. Then she returned to the campfire and dumped the pieces into the heating kettle.

Ruth had been fed, washed, and freshly diapered, and Charity was in her nightgown, waiting for supper. Hannah returned to the creek to wash the last traces of rabbit from her hands and cry in private. Unexpected kindness was hard to take.

While the meat cooked, Hannah poured a cup of coffee and leaned against the side of the nearest wagon. A few things had been removed from the wagons to allow room for blankets to be spread in spaces barely large enough to sleep in. They had planned the loading carefully with that in mind.

It was chilly, but Hannah was too tired to look for her shawl. The stars were out, and the sun was only a smear of gray to the west. Soon the moon would be up.

Ruth commenced to fuss again, and Hannah took her from Hilda and paced around the near vicinity of the fire, humming a lullaby and rubbing the baby's back. It didn't take long to get her to sleep. Hannah planted a kiss on the dark head before tucking her under a warm blanket in the girls' wagon.

When the dishes were done, the evening was actually pleasant. Erik pulled out the map. It didn't have a scale of miles on the bottom, like the fancy maps in books, but he knew the dimensions of the territory, and with an agreed upon guess of six miles they'd made that day, he figured out the ratio of miles to map size and carefully marked and dated their progress. If they could average ten miles a day, it would take them another seventeen days.

They were traveling, to start with, along the rails to the west. The going was relatively easy. Eventually, they would angle off to the north and northwest. Erik wanted to strike for the beginnings of the James River. There were no mountains or canyons to cross, so maybe they could do better than ten miles a day. They weren't sure exactly what to expect, as it was land not fully explored and mapped.

Hannah sat in the grass by the fire, and Charity climbed onto her lap. She fell asleep, but Hannah continued to hold her, too tired to make the effort to get up and put her to bed.

Jacob's laughter broke the comfortable silence.

"What is so funny?" his wife demanded, tired and seeing nothing amusing in any of this.

"A month ago, I never would've thought I would turn sodbuster!"

"Sodbuster?" Erik asked.

"A derogatory term for farmers—used by hunters and trappers who feel that farmers are ruining the land."

"And you resent being a sodbuster?"

"Only because I thought it would be boring. Now I'm

eager to give it a try."

Erik came to lift Charity from Hannah's lap and put her to bed, then he suggested prayers. Hilda and Halvor quietly retired to their wagon.

The night was divided into three parts. Each of the men would take a turn keeping watch, rotating so the same person didn't continually get stuck with the middle watch and interrupted sleep.

It had been a long day. Erik and Hannah rolled a bedroll out in the grass by the fire, and Hannah crawled in fully clothed but for her shoes. She immediately fell asleep on Erik's shoulder, safe and content to be near him.

Minutes later, so it seemed, Halvor was waking Erik. It was only a couple of hours until daylight.

Hannah didn't sleep so well after he got up. She would doze and wake again after only a few minutes. When Erik stoked the fire and put on the coffee pot, she gave up trying.

She rolled up and stowed the bedroll, then went to the creek in the early light for a wash. By the time the others got up, she had a stack of pancakes ready and more cooking.

"Do ve haf a gunny sack?" Erik asked when he refilled his cup.

"Yes."

"Hard to get to?"

"Not too hard."

Within a short time she had found the rough burlap bag and given it to him. He called Lisa over.

"Today, I vant you to valk. Collect dry dung in this." He handed her the empty sack. "For burning. There are no trees."

The girl's eyes showed her horror. "Vit my hands?!"

"Ya, my little princess, vith your hands."

"But, Papa—" she protested.

60

He cut her off abruptly in Norsk, and she obediently took the bag. Her face, however, still registered an indignant sulk.

"What on earth did you say to her?" Hannah asked when she'd gone, and before she thought that he may not want her to know.

"I told her she vas not too old to spank, and if she did not mind me, she vould have no choice but to valk for a few days, becoss she vill not vant to be sitting. I spoke in Norsk becoss I vas scolding her in front of somevun."

His blue eyes softened when they met hers. "You are their mama now. You spank them or scold them if they need it." With that, he went off to hitch the teams.

The consideration he'd shown to Lisa amazed her. Some new facet of his personality was always being revealed, impressing her, astounding her. She returned to the campfire area in time to hear him ask her mother if she could possibly take Ruth for part of the day. "It is hard for Hannah," he was saying, "to tend both girls and drife the vagon, too."

"I'm sorry I didn't think of it myself," her mother replied. "I sit there taking up space on the bench while Jacob drves. I could be doing something useful."

So it was established that Ruth would ride with the Campbells in the afternoons, when the little ones were the crabbiest and did better apart.

* * *

The morning passed easily. Ruth took a nap. The children ate crackers and played with the puppy. In the afternoon, Charity climbed onto the seat by Hannah for a chat.

Hannah pronounced her words carefully and slowly, hoping Charity's English would improve.

"Vat are clouds?"

"They are made of water."

"Vater? In da sky?"

"Yes. That's why we have rain."

"Vat are dose spots on your nose?"

"Freckles. They are only spots of darker skin that some people have."

"I like you."

"Thank you. I like you, too."

"May I have a cracker?"

"Yes."

Charity was back on the seat soon, with crumbs on her dress and dirty fingers.

"Dere is Papa!" A chubby finger pointed to where Erik had wandered off to the right after a pig.

She slept for a while with her head on Hannah's leg. She woke up and rubbed her eyes, then proceeded to locate John and Lisa. "Vat does Lisa haf?" she asked.

The bag was quite full, dragging behind Lisa.

"Fuel," Hannah answered.

Charity asked for no more explanation.

Lisa was tiring. When Hannah called to her, Erik turned to look, but he didn't seem to mind Hannah's pausing long enough to haul the girl and her burden up into the wagon.

Toward evening, she saw Erik aim his rifle and fire. He went to where a small, brown something lay in the grass and stooped for it. Twice more he fired. When he called a halt, Hannah expected him to hand her more rabbits.

To her surprise, he showed up not much later and gave her three prairie chickens—ready for the pot. How did he know? He bent a finger and caressed her cheek, gave a tender smile, and went his way to the multitude of chores that awaited.

* * *

The land they were now crossing had a few low, gentle hills covered in thick, long grass. There were wild flowers. The coulees still carried some of the spring runoff, but they were shallow and easy to cross. There were a lot of sloughs.

Cattails rimmed the little ponds, and red-winged black-birds darted in and out of the reeds. Coots and ducks swam on the surface, and there was usually a muskrat lodge out away from the shore. Hannah had seen a few of them break the water and swim. Only their little brown heads showed, with a "V" wrinkle on the water behind. Ducks and geese were on their way north. Large patches of ground were covered with geese, so many that it looked like snow. They were eating well on this trip, if nothing else.

There was plenty of time, between Charity's questions, for thinking. Hannah wondered how it was that Erik, the youngest man in the group, was the leader. He was the most qualified, and no one questioned it. And there was his hunting. True, there was plenty of game—almost any man could've kept them fed—but it was rare for him to come back with less game than she'd heard shots fired.

It became a contest for Charity to see how many animals she could spot. Badger, red fox, skunk, rabbit, meadowlark, tern. In the distance, they even saw a herd of buffalo.

* * *

Five nights out, Hannah was uneasy. The air smelled like rain. The muscled shoulder under her cheek tensed when the wind picked up. Clouds rolled over the quarter moon and thunder sounded in the distance.

"Luffly," Erik muttered. "I vas hoping ve vould get vet tonight."

His sarcasm was new to her.

Lightning flashed nearby, and the accompanying thunder was deafening. Quickly he got up and ran, dragging her with one hand and their bedding with the other. He scooted under John's wagon and spread the bedroll, then tugged Hannah under the wagon with him.

"Ve made it!"

Hannah settled herself, but sleep wouldn't come.

"Why did you start cleaning the game for me?" she asked.

"Yon said he saw that it made you sick. I am sorry that I didn't think uff you that first night. It is a bad job to haf to do, and I never thought about it being you I vas giving those rabbits to." He gave her arm a squeeze.

She snuggled closer. "Thank you for doing it for me since then," she said.

"You make me proud—" He stopped suddenly and sat up, bumping his head on the axle. He uttered a word that could only be an expression of complete irritation in Norwegian.

"Are you all right?"

"No!" He reached for her hand, and stuck it in the blankets on his side. They were wet. The wagon had been stopped with that side on slightly higher ground. If they stayed there, they would soon both be soaked.

"Go sleep with the girls."

"What about you?"

"I will get in vith Yon, but I von't sleep. Even in a whole bed, he kicks me all night."

"Poor thing!" She kissed his forehead in playful sympathy.

"Go!" he growled, but there was a smile in his voice.

Chapter 5

When they stopped the next evening, Hannah was as tired and miserable as she thought it was possible for a human to be. The night before had been cramped and chilly and damp, without enough blankets.

The girls hadn't slept as well as normal, either, because it was so crowded. The entire Nelsson family, with the exception of John, had been irritable all day. He was his usual, cheerful self, thriving on this life of endless walking and livestock herding.

Though she hadn't seen a mirror in a week, Hannah could imagine the circles under her eyes. And she was dirty. The day had been warm. Dusty, sweaty.

They'd halted for the night on the bank of the Sheyenne River. She wanted nothing more than to be able to escape long enough to take a bath. "Please, God," she said quietly, jumping from the wagon for a much-needed stretch, "let it be possible."

By now everyone was familiar with what needed doing. They were like well-rehearsed performers tiredly going through the play, doing what they were supposed to when they were supposed to do it. This evening, it was a drama of lethargy.

Hannah fed Ruth. She was warm, too, and teething, and did not want to eat. When Hannah moved her to a different position, her diaper leaked all over Hannah's dress. She sat, momentarily motionless, then stood up, holding the wet baby away from her.

"That's it!" she cried, and handed her to Erik. She'd been rained on, cold, kicked, kept awake, sweaty, dusty, hot. One of the horses had tried to bite her. Her hands were perpetually sore from the reins, as was her bottom from the hard seat. Being wet on was the last straw. "I'm going to take a bath!" She paused at the wagon only long enough to gather soap, towel, and clean clothes.

The water was cold, but it felt so good! She waded upstream, but stayed within easy screaming distance. Not that she thought she needed to; this trip had been anything but dangerous so far, unless one counted boredom and fatigue as dangers. But Erik would be angry if she weren't careful.

She stripped down to her camisole and pantaloons, then waded in. First she scrubbed her dirty clothes, then made her way to a nearby bush, feeling her way with her toes across the rocks and grass and mud of the bottom. She spread her clothes out to dry on the branches.

She waded until she found a relatively deep spot and dived under, taking care not to lose her soap. She came up with a sputter. It was not only cold, it was very cold. Quickly she soaped her hair and body, then rinsed. She didn't want to get out, even though her lips were probably blue. Getting out meant going back, returning to the monotonous nightmare of chores, driving, chores, sleeping.

66

A big stick floated by her arm, and she pushed it away. Only it wasn't a stick, and it wasn't floating. It was swimming. The frightened snake curled around the only solid thing available—her other arm. It was just a garter snake, but it was the biggest garter snake she had ever seen!

She screamed and Erik, coming at a run, arrived in time to see her throw it and run, sobbing and clumsy, to the water's edge. Not caring that she was cold and drenched, she threw herself at him, unable to get close enough or get the scaly, writhing feeling off her arm.

He hugged her with one arm, speaking soothing words in Norsk. He might be saying she was a silly crybaby for all she knew, but what did it matter as long as he held her?

His free hand suddenly tightened on his rifle, and the tension communicated to Hannah. She looked up and saw on the opposite bank five Indians on small horses. All of them were young men. Warriors.

The unfortunate snake slithered into the grass on their side. One of them watched it disappear, then his black eyes met Hannah's. There was the slightest quiver of a laugh on his mouth, but nothing friendly was in his eyes.

She crept behind Erik, and stood on tiptoe to peer over his shoulder. *Jesus, protect us!* she prayed silently.

With no apparent signal between them, the five ponies stepped forward together and crossed the creek.

The one Hannah had been staring at was their leader, or so she surmised. It was he who gestured to them to turn and walk to their camp. Erik walked in front of Hannah as they approached the camp, shielding her less-than-complete dress from the others' sight.

Margaret took in the situation at a glance. She came forward and wrapped a blanket around Hannah as the Indians came beyond the semi-circle of wagons into the camp.

The others stopped what they were doing and stood motionless.

The leader spotted Ruth. Slowly he rode his pony closer, to where an ashen-faced Lisa held her. The black eyes scanned the group.

"Who father?" His broken English took them by surprise.

"I am," Erik said.

Once more the black eyes, with a careful scrutiny that missed nothing, looked around. "Where squaw?"

There was no point in trying to explain the situation accurately.

"She returned to her people," Erik said.

The Indian measured Erik's words, then pointed to Ruth. "No want?"

"No, she didn't vant her."

Again he inspected the baby, who gurgled at him unafraid.

"No be white. Be Lakota." He reached for Ruth. Lisa shrank from him instinctively.

Instantly, Jacob moved to intercept the Indian's action, and at the same time, Erik pointed his rifle directly at the Indian leader. Hannah hadn't had time to blink before her father sank to the ground with an arrow through his leg, moaning in pain. Two more arrows and a musket were trained on Erik, and the Indian with the empty bow had a new arrow ready in almost the same instant.

The bargain was clear to them all. The Indians could have Ruth. Easily. There was no question who would win a battle between the two groups.

Hannah's lungs refused to function. There was a vise around her chest, and her heart hammered so that it made her throat tighten.

How could this be happening? Her father was injured, and she could lose both Erik and Ruth, all because of her. If she hadn't gone for a bath . . . if she hadn't screamed because of a snake that wasn't even poisonous . . . this wouldn't be happening.

"Please, God, please, God," she murmured, hardly realizing what she was saying.

Slowly, with an arrogant disdain for death, the Indian turned to stare at Erik and the muzzle of his gun. She could see the grudging admiration in his flint-hard eyes, and she could see him weighing the odds, deciding if the baby was worth this.

The brown hand withdrew, unhurried, and an unspoken command to the painted pony sent it toward Erik. Hannah was still hovering in fear near his arm. The Indian leaned forward from the horse's back to tip up her chin.

"Look like fog on water," he said, looking right at her eyes. His next words were to Erik, though he didn't remove his gaze from Hannah's wide, gray eyes. "I give five ponies."

The hand at her chin wasn't restricting, but she couldn't move any more than if he had her chained in place. She swallowed hard.

"No."

The brave turned toward Erik, and Erik returned the black gaze and spoke. "She is new. I like her."

They stared for what seemed like hours, neither of them willing to back down.

Wordlessly Hannah prayed. Her tongue wouldn't have worked anyway.

The Indian straightened on his horse. "She make laugh," he said. "You keep."

Without a further word they rode off in the same unhurried synchrony in which they had come.

Margaret and Hilda scurried to see how bad Jacob's leg was, while Erik led Hannah to the fire. When he'd gotten her a campstool to sit on, he left to have a look at the leg, too.

Hannah sat and shivered, ignoring all the noise and flying questions, listening for a verdict about her father. She,

69

Hannah, had caused this. How could she ever make it up to him?

The arrow had gone clean through. Halvor broke it in two and pulled out the shaft. As soon as Erik was satisfied that Margaret knew what she was doing in washing and bandaging the wound, he returned to Hannah.

"Nothing like a scare to make you forget a scare, is there?" he said.

She'd forgotten the snake. Now she shuddered, remembering its wet, scaly weight. Her teeth started chattering. She was wet and cold, but most of her misery was caused by guilt.

"I get your clothes, ya?" He disappeared into the twilight. How could it still be so light? The whole thing seemed like it had taken a very long time, but it must have been only a few minutes.

Lisa brought Hannah a cup of coffee, which she drank gratefully. Then Hannah started to comb out the long, still-wet tangles.

Prayers that night included thanks for protection.

Later, dry but unable to get warm, and still feeling guilty, Hannah moved closer to her husband. All was quiet in the night but the noises of crickets, frogs, and a far-off coyote.

"You are better now?"

"Just cold." She said no more, but she felt so bad that she couldn't continue to hold it inside. She had to talk to someone.

"Oh, Erik, I feel so horrible!"

"Vy?"

"My father got hurt, and we could've lost Ruth, and you could've been killed, and it's all my fault!"

"Your fault? How is it your fault?"

"If I hadn't screamed, those Indians never would have come."

"That is not true. They haf been following us for two days."

She sat halfway up. "Two days?"

"Ya."

She relaxed again. She could ask why he didn't tell her, but she already knew the answer. Why should he worry her or the children, when there was nothing they could do anyway?

It wasn't her fault.

"So why," she asked, "did you let me go off like that?"

"That is vat I ask myself. I did not think you vould go so far. I thought you only meant to vash. Still, I should've made sure uff vat you intended to do. Ven I think vat could've happened! They could've taken you! I should've told you uff the danger, and made sure you did not go so far that I could not see you."

"You were only trying to keep me from worrying. You did what you thought was best. It turned out fine."

"Thanks to God, not me."

"And I suppose that wasn't you I saw stand up to five armed Indians single-handed? I thought you were wonderful!"

He laughed quietly.

"What's so funny?"

"He vas right. You make me laugh."

"At what?"

He was laughing harder now. "You should've seen yourself throw that snake!"

"You beast!" She slapped his shaking chest, about as effectively as Ruth's little fists would do. "How can you laugh at me?"

"You are funny!"

"Well," she conceded, "I did manage to supply an amusing suppertime story."

"Stop that giggling and go to sleep!" Jacob said in the darkness.

71

Hannah's heart filled with joy that he felt up to teasing.

"Come here, Fog on Vater," Erik whispered, holding her close. He kissed each eyelid. "They are vorth no less than six ponies. Now mind your papa and go to sleep. I vill keep avay the snakes and the Indians."

* * *

Two days later they crossed the James River and turned to follow its west bank north. Hannah watched the hills and grass and flowers and sloughs, and her appreciation for this land grew. The little band of travelers were insignificant specks on a flat dish of land, under a sky that had no end.

Mid-morning four days later, they came over a hill and saw where the river curved to the west. Erik stopped and surveyed the area while he waited for Hannah to catch up. "Vat do you think?" he asked her.

She was ready to stop anywhere, but she looked around critically. Was this where she wanted to live for the rest of her life? All around was the tall grass, dotted with wildflowers, in low rises for as far as she could see. The little river cut through, and a stand of spindly trees stood along it. She tried to picture it in winter. What would it be like with people and buildings and trees?

"Where is the nearest town?" she asked.

"If ve are vere I think ve are, it is Bismarck, about fifty miles to the southvest."

"And trees?"

"North. At least a veek. I'm not sure."

If he was satisfied, she was. It was as pretty as any other spot they'd come across. "Looks good to me," she said.

Halvor halted his team on Erik's other side, and they discussed the area for a few minutes. Not in English, of course, but Hannah was too weary to listen or care.

By evening they had selected a site, set up tents, and picketed the animals. A small tent for the Campbells faced east. Across a space of about thirty feet, the Johannsons' tent faced west. Facing south, and forming a third wall of a square, was a larger tent for the Nelssons.

The wagons had been unloaded, and the tents were crowded. Hannah set up her bed in one corner, complete with dust ruffle. It looked out of place there in the cramped tent, but if it had to take up space, it was only logical to use it. She'd had enough of a bedroll on the ground. The washstand stood beside it, another welcome sight. It was a relief to be able to wash somewhere besides a creek or river.

It was in this larger tent that the men sat around a table which had been in the Campbells' kitchen in Fargo. While they drank coffee, they worked out how they would go to file their claims and bring back building materials.

Hannah left them sitting there and crawled into bed. A month ago, she wouldn't have dreamed of going to bed in the same room as a man other than her husband or father. But two and a half weeks of sleeping by the fire had made that sense of "fishbowl living" almost disappear. Anyway, Halvor never spoke to her and ignored her totally unless it was her turn to cook. She could be another table for all the notice he gave her.

The next morning, Erik and Jacob left for Bismarck. It was a period of welcome boredom for Hannah. They needed to start a garden, but they wouldn't be plowing up any land until they were sure where the claims would lie.

It was also a period of rest. In the warm part of the day, the children played in the river. Hannah sewed a dress for Ruth and began another for Charity.

John was always busy. The world was full of delights. Two dogs, a puppy, and the kittens were old enough to play. One of the cows had a calf. There were chickens to feed, eggs to collect, cows to milk. And besides the animals they brought along, there was a multitude of creatures outside. He brought in a constant stream, asking if he could keep them. A frog, a large turtle, a salamander, a snake. No, no, no, no.

Then he brought in a baby raccoon, and Hannah, tired of saying no, gave in. With leathery hands, the little creature felt Hannah's face, chattering at her as though she should understand.

The raccoon got into more trouble than Ruth, if that were possible. One morning Hannah awoke to find the coffee beans spilled all over. Another time it got into her bottle of lavender water, and the tent smelled so strong that they had to loosen the sides of the canvas to let it air.

They had more time for cooking, and did some baking. Fresh bread. A cake. It was paradise.

After nine days, Erik and Jacob returned. The wagons were full of lumber, glass windows, door knobs, and nails. There were new pants for John, fabric for clothes and curtains. There was more food, even some fruit.

They had a bit of a celebration, with cake and coffee, to mark the beginning of their homestead. Then they marked out their claims and decided where they would put barns and houses and gardens.

Before Hannah knew it, Erik was gone again, this time with Halvor to file his claim. He hoped to sell the extra wagon and team.

Nine more days. This time, when he came back, he stayed awhile.

The livestock needed protection, so first the men built barns. They put them in the side of a hill, with extending walls made of sod squares cut from the prairie. It took two weeks to make all three.

Erik would work until dark, then eat, take a swim in the river, and fall immediately asleep.

Next they started plowing, turning over a section large enough for a community garden and a test patch of wheat.

Work, eat, and sleep. Hannah was lonely for Erik's company, but he ignored her. He ignored the girls as well. John he talked to, because he was helping him.

One night, he came in from the field early, and Hannah's hopes soared.

"Make coffee," he ordered. "Ve must talk about houses now."

But "ve" was the three men, not her, and they talked late into the night around the table. Hannah hid her face in her pillow so they would not hear her cry.

Next morning, the men left to get wood. They took John, who was ecstatic, and left the dogs and a rifle. The women would sleep together in the large tent while they were gone.

* * *

Hannah woke up with a familiar wave of nausea, and admitted to herself what she'd been suspecting for a while. She was pregnant.

For a little while she lay there, waiting for the sickness to pass. So far it always had, and she hoped it would continue to, so she could keep her secret. Erik should know first.

She didn't know when they would be back from the hills, and she didn't know if they would turn right around and go back for more wood when they did return. Erik never talked to her anymore. Her father got to see him and talk to him much more than she did. She resisted the urge to scream and beat her pillow.

Late that morning, Charity and Ruth were playing on a blanket in the sun while the three women and Lisa pulled weeds in the garden. Suddenly the wagons rattled into view.

Hannah was euphoric, dizzy with joy, watching Erik grow larger in her field of vision. Surely, that weak-kneed sensation should be gone by now, but there it was. Did he feel anything even remotely like this, knowing he would see her within the next minute or two?

Sometimes she thought he regretted marrying her. She didn't want to think so. As far as she knew, nothing had changed since he'd hugged her so tight, calling her "Fog on Vater." That night, she'd been so sure he loved her. But since then, particularly since they'd taken up tent living, she had had her doubts.

How would he take her news?

The girls clambered around him, demanding attention, which he gave them. She was glad to see it. She knew they, too, had been perplexed by his aloof manner. How would he greet her? Was he just so busy and so tired that he had no energy left for anyone?

Picking up Ruth, she went to see him and stood quietly, waiting to take her cue from him. Ruth reached for him, gurgling with excitement. He took her and gave her a brief cuddle and a toss in the air. He brushed his lips over Hannah's temple, then walked to the tent area with Charity on his neck and Ruth on his hip so he could still hold Lisa's hand and have an arm free to put around Hannah.

Her misgivings took wings. He *was* happy to be home, to see them. To see her.

The area all the tents faced was where they had their cooking fire. It had become a sort of extended family, open-air living room. Everyone sat around and listened while the men told of their trip. Erik and Jacob described the hills, trees, and wildlife they'd seen. Halvor, who could understand most of what was said, but who adamantly refused to speak English, would occasionally put in a word or two, which Erik or Hilda would translate.

It was good to rest, but the wagons called. There was a lot of wood to unload.

After supper the men milked the cows and fed and watered the other animals. The women washed dishes and got the children ready for bed.

In their own tent there were prayers, then Erik read to the children in Norwegian. Ruth, then Charity, fell asleep, but John and Lisa listened intently, occasionally gasping or laughing. Hannah closed her eyes and enjoyed the baritone melody of his voice.

When John fell asleep, Erik closed the book. "Lisa," he said softly. "Hannah is going to take a valk vith me. If you haf trouble, call for Yacob or Halvor."

Hannah gaped at him stupidly. He held out a hand, and she took it.

"Did you miss me?" His arm was around her waist while they walked.

"Yes. Are you going again?"

"Ya. But not until ve run out uff logs. Ve vill start a cabin for your parents tomorrow. I think maybe ve haf enough logs for both uff the little cabins."

They crossed a hill and rounded the stand of trees by the river. On a slight rise, they sat in the grass. Hannah bent her legs to one side under her skirt and leaned a hand in the cool grass. Erik lay on his back, using her lap for a pillow.

"Thank you for being patient," he said. "I am trying to get those cabins built as kvickly as I can, so ve vill not alvays haf an audience. I should not haf to valk out here vith you yust to talk to you vithout anyvun listening."

"Sounds like you have something particular in mind to talk about."

"No. I yust vant to talk to you. There is alvays somevun around. I am very tired uff alvays being vatched."

But now that he had the opportunity, he didn't talk. He fell asleep.

Hannah stroked his hair and watched him. The moon had risen and reflected a long path on the water, casting enough light to see his face. She would never tire of looking at him, noticing every nuance of change in muscle and

77

skin. It was hard to believe he was real. A human, not a statue. The silvery light added to the illusion that he was carved in marble, and not a flesh and blood man.

Soon her legs were killing her. She had to move. She shook him gently, reluctant to wake him. He worked too hard. She had a different reason for being tired, and now was her chance to tell him.

"Erik?"

"Hm?"

"Are you awake?"

"Ya."

"I mean completely awake?"

He sat up and drew a deep, weary breath. "Vat is so important?"

She felt guilty. Her legs could have lasted a little while yet.

"We're going to have a baby." Uncertain how he would react, she allowed her voice to reveal neither joy nor regret.

It took him a second to assimilate the information. Then he asked incredulously, "Already?"

Hannah pulled her legs up and folded her arms over their tops. "That's what I thought, too."

"You don't sound happy about it."

"I'm happy." She turned her head so she could watch him. "I was afraid you wouldn't be. It's a bad time. It's so soon. Ruth is so young. There's so much work to do."

"Hannah, I am happy. It vill be a beautiful baby! Does your mama know? She vill be excited."

"I haven't told anyone yet. I wanted to tell you first."

He held her against him, and she looked up into his eyes, dark in the shadows of night.

"I hope it's a boy!" she said in a rush. "And I hope he looks just like you! Oh, Erik, I love you! And can we name him Erik?"

He didn't speak at first, but crushed her in arms that

78

barely allowed her to breathe. Then in an emotional voice, he said, "You vant to name him Erik?"

"Yes," she said with a tiny frown of confusion. Didn't he understand what she was saying? With more conviction she repeated, "Erik, I love you!"

The words had tumbled out without forethought before, and she wanted to be sure he knew she meant it. She didn't deserve him. He might resent the fact that she loved him, or pity her, but there was no way she could hide it, so she might as well say it aloud.

"Hannah, *min elskede!*" His words were little more than a breath on her face.

"What does that mean?"

He didn't answer.

"Is it a pet name in Norwegian, like Fog on Water?"

"Something like that."

Min elskede. Hilda would know what it meant, but she couldn't ask her. Hilda didn't need to know their private conversations. And Erik apparently didn't want her to know. Considering his strange behavior, it might be better not to. She filed it away in her memory.

"We should get back," she said. "Ruth might wake up. She's teething again."

* * *

June was fading into July. It would be another hot day. Hannah stood outside washing the breakfast dishes. Her mother and Hilda were working in the garden. The men were starting the second cabin, the one for the Johannsons, about a quarter of a mile to the west. Her parents' cabin, already finished, was a quarter mile to the east. They had all claimed adjoining land so they would be close enough to help each other.

She was surprised at how fast the construction was going. With planked floors and glass windows, she had thought it would take longer.

79

As soon as the Campbells had settled into their new home, John had moved into their tent, alleviating the crowding a bit. Lisa and Charity would be moving to their own "room," too, as soon as the next cabin was finished.

Hannah almost didn't want the next cabin to get done, for then there would be no reason for Erik to ask her to go for a walk. It was the only time they really talked, without all the cares and interruptions of their world.

"Hannah?" Lisa stood by her. "Do you have a second name?"

"Yes. It's Mary. So my whole name is Hannah Mary Campbell Nelsson."

"Is dat vat you vill name da baby? Mary?"

Everyone knew about the baby, and they were all counting the days until January. Hilda, while happy for them, was envious. She and Halvor had been married for five years but had no children. Hannah had added their wish for a child to her prayers.

"I haven't thought about a name for a girl yet. Why do you ask?"

"I haf my mama's second name. She vas Marta Eleesabett Nelsson."

Hannah tried to make her smile pleasant. "That's a pretty name." She preferred to pretend there had never been such a person as Marta Elizabeth Nelsson. To make conversation, she asked, "What is your second name?"

"Pauline."

"Is Paul Erik's second name?" She should've known his middle name before now, but she'd never thought to ask.

"He has no second name. Yust Erik."

"Are you named for the apostle, then?"

"I don't know. Vas Paul a very important apostle?"

"He certainly was."

"Maybe dat's vy, den. I haf vundered vy Mama and Papa named us dat."

"Us?"

"Ya. I am Pauline, Yon is Paul, and Charity is Paulette."

With a wet plate in her hand, Hannah faced Lisa. That didn't make sense. "Are you sure?"

Lisa looked at her, insulted. "Ya, I am sure. May I go down by da river now?"

"Yes."

How very odd. Hannah thought about it while she finished the dishes, but it was soon forced from her mind by other demands. Ruth needed feeding and changing, then it would be time to take a dinner to the cabin-builders.

Just when Hannah was ready to leave with a basket of food, a stranger rode up. He was bearded, none too clean, and chewing the end of a cigar, but the dark blue eyes under the shadow of his hat brim were friendly. The half of his mouth not occupied with the cigar smiled at her from the top of his large, black horse.

"Mornin,' ma'am," he drawled.

"Good morning, sir. Have you traveled far? I was just taking dinner to my husband. Are you hungry?"

Hospitality was the rule of the west. Polite treatment of women was another, so Hannah wasn't afraid. A man could get hung for mistreating a lady almost as quickly as for stealing a horse. Besides, a scream would bring her mother and Hilda at once—and Hilda had a rifle.

"I could use a bite if it's no hardship on you." He stepped gracefully from the horse, accompanied by the creak of leather and the smell of sweat, both horse and human.

Hannah dug two sandwiches, a precious apple, and a handful of cookies from the basket and gave them to him. "There's coffee hot. Would you like a cup?"

"Thank you, yes. This looks tasty. I haven't put you out any?"

"No," she assured him. "I made plenty." She turned

81

toward the tent. "Lisa! Bring out a mug, please."

While he ate, they made small talk about the weather and the homesteaders. He said folks were pouring into the territory and it wouldn't be long before they had neighbors.

"Is that what brings you, Mr. . . . ?"

"Cooper. Charles Cooper."

"Mr. Cooper. Are you looking for land to file on?"

"No, ma'am." His smile was much nicer without the cigar. "I'm delivering a letter. Fella named Nelsson is supposed to be livin' in these parts." He pulled a dirty envelope from his shirt pocket. "Erik Nelsson. This letter's gone from a place called Bergen in Norway to Minneapolis, to Fargo, and Bismarck. It sat at the post office there for weeks. I was going to Grand Forks, so I said I'd have a look around for him. Do you know him?"

"He is my husband."

"Well, then," he grinned. "I expect I can leave this with you." He gave it to her. "Thank you for the food."

"Thank *you*, Mr. Cooper, for going out of your way to deliver this letter. You are welcome to stay the night if you like."

"No, thank you, Mrs. Nelsson. I can still make ten miles today."

He mounted his horse and rode off as Hannah called after him. "Thank you! You're welcome anytime!"

As soon as he was gone, Hannah set out for the cabin site at a trot. "Erik!"

They were cutting a log the proper length and stopped when she came.

"Vat took you so long? I am starving."

"A stranger brought this!" She gave him the letter.

He held it for a moment in disbelief, then tore it open.

"Who is it from?" she asked.

"My sister."

"Your sister?" She hadn't even known he had a sister, or any family, for that matter.

He sat down, leaning against the partial wall, and read.

"Here's your dinner, Papa, Halvor." Hannah set the basket down and hurried to follow Erik.

His eyes moved to the date at the top.

"She is here, in America! They are moofing to Minneapolis. She vants to see me. She thinks I am in Minneapolis, but it is not so far. She could take the train to Bismarck. If I knew ven to expect her, I could take the vagon and get them for a visit. Her and her baby and husband."

He covered his face with his hands for a minute, trying to take it all in. "I can't beleaf it! I haf not seen her for more than tvelf years! She vas only elefen ven I left, younger than Lisa is now! And she is grown up and has a baby! I can't beleaf it! Maren, here, in this country!"

"I didn't know you had a sister. I never thought about your family or where you came from. Tell me about it?"

He didn't look sure that he wanted to.

"You can't let me continue to believe that God made you full grown and dropped you in Fargo, can you?"

He almost smiled, and Hannah pressed her advantage. "Were you once a little boy?"

He laughed. "You do manage to get your vay, don't you? And you make me laugh, so I vill haf to keep you."

"Don't evade the question, Mr. Nelsson. Do you have other family? Tell me about Norway."

"Norvay is a beautiful country, but it is hard."

"Wait!" She ran to get the basket. Jacob and Halvor were resting in the shade on the other side of the cabin. She smiled to think of the English and charades the two used to communicate when Erik wasn't around.

"*Vait?*" He reached for a sandwich. "You go through so much effort to talk me into telling you my boring past, and then you say 'Vait?' "

"I can't let you perish from the effort," she said sweetly, and dropped to the ground to sit with him.

He picked up where he'd left off. "There are mountains and many trees. Lakes like blue glass, deep fjords. It is beautiful."

"So why did you leave?"

"The soil is hard. Farms are small and vorn out. My brother has the farm. It vill not support two families."

"You have a brother also?"

"Two. And vun sister. Per is the oldest. He is thirty-fife now, two years older than me. He has the farm. He is married and has three sons."

"What does he look like?"

"Full uff kvestions. If you vere an Indian, you vould go through two or three names a year. He is shorter than I am, an inch or two. His hair is lighter, nearly vite.

"Amund is thirty-vun now. He is yust recently married and he vorks in a factory in Bergen. He could be my tvin in looks, but his eyes are very dark blue, like the night.

"Maren is tventy-three. She is the baby. Her hair is the color uff butter. Last time I saw her, she vas a little girl in a pink dress, vaving to me from the front uff the house as I left." He drew a shaky breath. "And my parents are dead. That's all there is."

"I'm sorry I made you think of these things."

"The letter vould've made me think, anyvay. But now, I must get back to vork. *Takk for maten.*"

Takk for maten, she'd learned, meant "Thanks for the food." Right now it also meant "End of conversation. Go home."

Another question came to her later, while she worked. That night she knew he was not yet asleep, and she quietly spoke.

"Why did you tell me you would send the children to your aunt if I wouldn't marry you? They have closer family."

"Becoss I think she is the only vun who vould take all

three uff them." He rolled away from her, and she asked no more questions.

Chapter 6

Over supper, Erik wondered out loud whether he should go to Bismarck to check the mail. It had been several weeks since Maren had written the letter, and she should be in Minneapolis by now. She would've discovered that he was no longer there, and she might've written again with an address at which he could reach her. Then again, perhaps she would lose hope of ever finding him and not write.

But there was really no choice. They had to finish the Johannsons' cabin, then it would be time for haying. The grass that grew in profusion in all directions was theirs to cut and dry and store to feed the stock through the winter. After that, maybe he could take the time needed to go to town.

"She will write again," Hannah said later, when they were alone.

"How do you know?"

"Because you left a forwarding address. If she wrote all the way from Norway that she wants to see you, she won't give up without looking into where you went. She will write again, and the letter will follow you to Bismarck.

"I'm anxious to meet her," she added. "I never had a sister. I had two brothers."

"You did? No vun ever told me that."

"You never asked. Like I never asked about your family. James died when he was two and I was four. He drowned. I don't remember him. Joseph died when he was only one day old. It was a blood problem. I was five, and I don't remember him, either.

"They are the reason, I think, why Mama dotes on the children so, and why she is so happy about little Erik, here." "Little Erik" was just making Hannah's dress too tight to button at the waist.

"Vill she be so happy if 'Little Erik' is a girl?" he asked. "Vill you?"

"Certainly! But I still hope she looks like you."

The callouses on the thumb he used to caress her cheek were pleasantly rough, like a cat's tongue. "As long as she has your eyes," he said.

* * *

Charity whimpered in the night. Thinking it was a nightmare, Hannah got up to check on her. The little girl had them before. Holding her for a little while always helped her fall back asleep.

But it was not a nightmare, it was a fever. Charity's forehead was burning.

Hannah got a pan of cool water and some rags to wipe her with, and started praying.

"Vat is wrong?" Erik lit a candle.

He came and felt the small, hot face. Hannah saw the worry in his eyes and remembered that his first wife had died from a fever. And Marta had had a doctor.

What reassurance could she give him? There were no guarantees. They could pray, they could keep her cool, they could try to get her to drink. The rest was in God's hands.

In the morning, Margaret and Hilda hovered around. Hannah warned them that it might be contagious, but they reasoned that they'd been around Charity the previous day. If they were going to catch it, they would anyway.

Jacob and Halvor went to work, telling Erik to stay with his daughter. For a time, he did. Then he took his scythe and went out to cut hay.

"Time vill go kvicker if I am vorking," he said. "I am useless to a child vith a grandmother and two mothers. I can pray yust as vell outside."

Hannah took a nap in the afternoon so she could sit up with Charity through the night after Hilda and her mother went home.

In the evening Erik took care of Ruth, then paced around. Finally he fell asleep, to Hannah's relief. She could understand his worry, but the constant pacing was irritating.

During the night, Charity began shivering. Now the job was to keep her warm. Hannah wrapped her in a blanket and held her, wearing a path on the dirt floor of the tent. What she would give for a rocking chair!

Just before dawn Charity quit whimpering and fell into a peaceful sleep. She was cool to the touch. Thank God!

What Hannah wanted to do now was sleep herself. She sat on the floor and leaned her head against a trunk. Her eyes felt gritty. She let them close, but she didn't let herself sleep. It was almost morning, and there were too many things to do. There was laundry. Some of the early vegetables were ready to pick. That meant canning. Then there were always the daily chores.

"How is she?" Erik asked.

"Better," Hannah answered without opening her eyes. "She just now fell asleep."

He knelt on the pile of blankets on the floor that was Charity's bed to see for himself. Hannah was aware of his movement, though she didn't look. A moment later she was startled by his touch on her hair.

"Thank you, Hannah."

Hannah didn't want to take credit for doing what anyone would've done. "I'm just thankful that she's well," she said.

"I don't mean yust for sitting up vith Charity vile she vas ill. I mean for everything. Vat vould I do vithout you?"

"Marry Jenny Smith?"

He frowned. "That is not funny. I am serious. And I never considered marrying Yenny Smit."

"You didn't?" Her eyes were open now.

He shook his head slowly, his eyes never leaving hers. "Not for a minute."

"But you said . . ."

"She vas recommended, that is true. But your smile is like sunshine. And don't tell your mama, but I don't like hair that bright red. Or green eyes either."

Her smile—like sunshine?—flashed at him. "Why?"

"They remind me of cats."

"You don't like cats?"

"Cats are fine as cats. Not as vomen."

"That's silly."

"Ya." He looked momentarily at Charity.

"You could use some sleep, too," he told her. "Vy don't you go to bed?"

"There's too much to do. And Mama and Hilda had to do all the gardening and cooking yesterday."

"I insist."

"You insist? What would you do if I refused?"

She hadn't been serious, but he was. "Don't make me

think uff something. Get to bed."

She slept for hours.

* * *

Charity and Ruth were both screaming. Hannah went to find out what the problem was. Charity was four now, and Ruth was ten months. They were best friends and worst enemies.

"What happened?" she asked, rounding the corner of the tent. Ruth was sitting on the ground. Charity was holding her head and howling.

"She pulled my hair!" Charity wailed. It was difficult to believe that less than two weeks ago, they'd wondered if she would live. Now she was jumping around like a frog and making enough noise for ten children.

"So why is she crying?" Hannah asked her.

Charity quit yelling and cast her eyes down, not as innocent as she wanted her stepmother to believe.

"Tell me," Hannah said.

"I knocked her down."

Ruth was just learning to walk. It didn't take much of a push to topple her. Hannah explained that Ruth was too little to understand that she'd hurt Charity, and that revenge wasn't what God wanted.

"Anybody home?" a voice called, interrupting her sermon.

Hannah went around to the front of the tent.

It was Charles Cooper, though she wouldn't have recognized him on a different horse. He'd washed and shaved, and he wore a new shirt and hat.

"Why, Mr. Cooper! Welcome! What brings you back?"

"Just moseying along, back to Bismarck." He jumped from the big horse, wearing a grin under the black mustache he'd kept when he'd shaved off his beard. Not a bad-looking man, actually. "Thought I'd stop by and see how the homesteadin' is going."

"Quite well, thank you. Can I offer you some coffee? Or perhaps you would prefer water on a day like today?"

"It's a scorcher, isn't it? Water would hit the spot."

He hitched his horse to a tent pole and followed her to the dipper and bucket in the shade.

"You are welcome to stay. I have several fresh perch I was going to fry for supper, and I just made an oatmeal cake this morning."

"That does sound tempting."

"I'm sure my husband would like to thank you personally for bringing him that letter. They're out haying, but he should be in soon."

"In that case, yes."

It would be good to hear another voice at suppertime, especially one that had news from Grand Forks and the world.

Lisa led Charity and carried Ruth over to be washed for supper.

"Yours?" Mr. Cooper asked. "You don't look old enough."

"Mine through marriage. And again, thank you. This is Elizabeth, and this is Charity. This—" she took the heavy baby from Lisa—"is Ruth."

"Adopted," she answered the politely unasked question that was written all over his face.

"No boys?"

"One. His father's shadow."

Hannah put Ruth down, set the frying pan over the fire, and flipped her braid over her shoulder. She should wear a bonnet. She knew her face and neck were turning brown, but she hating have the broad brim hinder her view. While the pan heated, she sliced bread. There were also potatoes baking in the coals, and fresh green beans.

"That looks good, Mrs. Nelsson."

"Well, we're glad to be able to offer you something in thanks. That was a very special letter you brought."

"Oh?" He seated himself on one of the campstools to watch her cook.

"From Erik's sister." She turned to Lisa, saying, "Please get out the plates and cups", then back to her guest. "He hasn't seen her for a long time, so he was very glad to hear from her."

"Then I'm doubly glad I managed to find you."

"Doubly?"

"It's always a pleasure to meet good folks. And you've fed me twice."

John came trudging up, tired and dirty.

"Where is your papa?" Hannah asked.

"He is coming."

"Then go wash for supper."

Suddenly finding new energy, John ran off. His "wash" always grew into a swim. Hannah watched him go, with his raccoon running behind, chattering angrily at John for going too quickly. She laughed.

"You love them, don't you?" Mr. Cooper asked. There was a certain amount of astonishment in his question.

"Sure I do."

"That's unusual for a stepmother. Or at least for a new stepmother. You are new—or am I getting too personal?"

It was impossible to be offended. "Just over three months."

"That's incredible. My stepmother hated me."

"I find that hard to believe, Mr. Cooper."

"Resented my presence, then. Though I admit her resentment was well-earned. I remember one time my brother and I climbed the oak tree up through her sitting room window and put frogs in her bathwater. You should have heard her scream!"

Hannah laughed with pleasure at the image just as Erik came around the side of John's tent.

Hannah noted the direction of Mr. Cooper's gaze and how his grin faded. She turned to see Erik.

93

He was dirty and sweaty. His shirt clung to him in wet patches. A trickle of sweat ran down the side of his face, and there were bits of hay in his hair. Even tired and dirty, he was an incredibly handsome man. He stopped and put one hand on a hip, running the back of the other over his forehead.

"Erik!" Hannah filled the dipper and took him a drink. "We have a guest for supper." She made a quick introduction. "Mr. Cooper is the one who brought your letter from Maren. He's on his way back to Bismarck."

Erik curved his arm around her waist while he drank and left it there, preventing her from returning the dipper. She was quite happy to remain by him.

"Twenty miles out uff your vay yust for a visit?" he asked skeptically.

"I'm not on a schedule. Just wanderin'. As I told your wife, I enjoy meeting good folks." He let a friendly, winning smile show a band of white under his moustache. "And I know the food is good here."

"That is true," Erik agreed, and kissed his wife.

Hannah was flabbergasted. In front of someone?!

"I am getting a clean shirt. Then I go to the river for a vash before supper." He went into the tent momentarily, then, shirt in hand, followed the path taken by John.

Hannah was not aware of the pink on her cheeks or the shine in her eyes while she watched him go. She returned to the fire to flip the last of the fish out onto a clean rag to drain.

"You can put your things in this tent," she said pointing to John's, "and sleep there."

"No, thank you, Mrs. Nelsson. I'll be on my way after supper."

Surprised, she glanced to the west. The sun would be down before they were done eating. Was he going to travel in the dark?

"It's not raining. I prefer the stars."

* * *

At supper they talked about the depression that had started the previous year. Hard pressed, people were going west in droves, pinning their hopes on the free land. Charles Cooper was able to converse knowledgeably with Erik about crops and soil quality. The talk moved around to the continuing "reconstruction" of the south, another subject he knew about. He'd grown up on a Virginia plantation. The house had been burned during the war and most of the land confiscated for taxes. His parents were now living in the foreman's house. The rest of the family had scattered.

"I should go back," he said when the night had grown late and the children were all asleep. "My father isn't well, last I heard. He needs help with what land is left." He folded his hands between his knees and stared at them.

"You've taught me something," he said. "A man doesn't need miles of land, slaves, and crystal on the table to be happy. Maybe I'll go home, settle down, and try to make up to Abigail for being so rotten to her for so many years." He glanced up at Erik to explain that Abigail was his stepmother. "For one thing, I could take her to church. I know she sets a store by that, and Father won't take her."

"That sounds like a good idea," Erik said. "Don't go to the church yust for her, though. He is not yust a God for old ladies." His next words were to Hannah.

"Can ve haf pancakes vith chokecherry syrup for breakfast?" He looked to Charles. "You are staying?"

From Erik, their guest accepted the invitation.

Hannah turned in, and Erik helped Charles set up his bedroll in John's tent. She was brushing out her hair when he came laughing into their tent.

"Tventy miles to visit good folks!" he said with a grin.

"What is so strange about that?"

"Vat is the American expression about a pig's eye?"

She set down the brush and twisted around to face him. "What are you getting at?"

"Hannah, my innocent!" He came and kissed the tip of her nose. "He rode that twenty miles to see you!"

"Me?" she squeaked. Her voice returned to normal. "That's ridiculous! I'm married! He knew that!"

"Maybe he vas hoping you vere not kvite so married. A voman stuck miles from anyvere vith an old vidower might enjoy the attention of a handsome young man."

Hannah drew her eyebrows together. It was possible. She recognized that there had been an immediate friendship between herself and Mr. Cooper, and she knew that there were people who didn't respect rings or vows.

Possible, but not likely. She didn't think he was that type. And if she'd never had a suitor so determined when she was single, it was ridiculous to believe one would go to such lengths for such an unlikely chance. She thought Erik's theory a bit farfetched.

"I'm glad he came, anyway. It's turned out well. And I hope he sticks to his plan and takes his stepmother to church. It might rub off."

"Ya. And if he really vants to settle down, I can testify that church is a good place to find a vife!"

* * *

It had been almost two weeks now since the second cabin was finished, and the Nelssons were living as a normal family, albeit still in tents. Even so, Erik had asked her to go for a walk once. She no longer even thought about whether or not she was pretty. He wasn't complaining, and he made her feel pretty, whether she was or not.

They would finish the haying today, Erik said. Then they would begin building their house. Hannah was anxious to move in. She was tired of living out of boxes and cooking over a fire. She frowned. That was a fact that wouldn't change soon, even if they did have a house. They had no woodstoves.

She and the girls walked the quarter mile to her parents' cabin.

"Come in!" her mother called at her knock. Margaret set aside the curtains she was making for the four windows. One faced each direction, so they could keep watch on the all-important sky.

The little girls played on the floor while Lisa sat in fascination, listening to the grown-up talk of babies and sipping her tea.

"That's a job I'm glad to see done!" Jacob said, walking in on the mother-daughter talk. "I've never been so itchy and sweaty in all my life."

"You are finished with the hay?"

"Yes, and I have to say it feels good to see the stacks by all the barns, ready for winter!"

"I should go home, then. Erik will be there."

"Come outside with me, first."

Full of curiosity, Hannah followed her father out and sat next to him on the riverbank.

"Happy?" he asked.

"Yes."

"Me, too. Didn't think I'd ever enjoy being a farmer, but it has its rewards. I was bored with both Fargo and the store." He stretched. "I'm forty-eight. I felt old there. Now I feel ten years younger. Must be the exercise."

Gray eyes met gray eyes. His creased at the corners. "We chose well with this Nelsson fella, didn't we?"

"We certainly did."

Jacob turned his gaze back to the river. A turtle slid off a rock into the water.

"What is this leading to, Papa?"

"Just a chat, so far." He patted her hand. "Remember when I went to Bismarck with Erik?"

"Yes?"

"Well, I didn't file a claim. I bought the land outright. Erik knows that. What he doesn't know is that I bought it in your name."

"My name?"

"I'd like to farm it until I get too old, or get tired of it. Legally, you could kick me off," he added with a little chuckle.

She made a face. "Why?"

"You'll have it someday, anyway, when I die. This way, you have something of value to give your husband. A dowry, or wedding present. At the time, I was thinking that I wanted you to have something of your own to fall back on if your husband turned out to be—how to put this delicately? Let's say that the ladies appreciate him. It takes a man strong in faith, or in love, or both, to ignore such offers." He held up a hand to stem her protest. "I thought from the start he was good, or I would've warned you against him. Now I see that his faith is genuine. But a father thinks of these things. Anyway, I wanted you to have it."

"Thank you, Papa." She hugged him. "Thank you for caring enough to 'think of these things.' But what do you mean about getting tired of farming? What would you do?"

"I'm not tired of it yet," he assured her. "But I know what I'd do. I'd open a store!"

She looked around. Nothing but grass, low hills, and the river. "A store?"

"It won't be like this for long, Hannah. I bet we'll have neighbors in less than a year. In five, there'll be a town around here. I could save folks a nine-day trip to Bismarck! Make a nice profit by bringing the supplies to them."

"I believe you're looking forward to it," she said with a smile.

"Sure." He grinned back. "But not yet. No customers."

Chapter 7

"H annah!" Erik called.

It was early, just after breakfast. He'd only gone out to whatever job he'd planned for the day a few minutes ago. Hannah was changing Ruth out of her nightgown.

He came into the big tent, looking for her.

"Pack," he ordered when he spotted her.

"Pack?" she repeated. "Pack what? Do you need a lunch?"

"No!" A grin broke across his face. "Clothes. Some for the girls, some for Yon. Some for us!"

"What are you talking about?"

"Enough for nine or ten days. Yon is staying vith Halvor, the girls with Maggie. You"—he lifted her completely off the ground and swung her around—"are coming to Bismarck vith me!"

Comprehension dawned, but she was afraid to believe what her ears were telling her.

"I thought I'd go alone, or maybe take Halvor. Then I thought it vould be more fun to take you. Stay in a hotel, eat in a restaurant. *Too bad I can't,* I thought. By vy not? There is no reason vy not, except to ask somevun else to vatch the children, so I did. You deserve a break, and you are going!"

* * *

The quiet was wonderful. No questions. No crying baby. No conversations between Lisa and John about the superiority of cats versus dogs, or whether a particular snake was four feet long or five.

Hannah closed her eyes. A bird was singing. The sun was warm, but not hot. Erik was by her side.

"How is Little Erik taking the ride?" he asked. "Ve can stop for a rest if you like."

"Little Erik is taking the ride just fine, and so is his mother." Her mouth curved up at the corners in contentment.

"Have you thought about names for a girl?"

"No. How about a Bible name?"

"If you like."

She thought for a while, then gave up. "I can only think of boy names. David, Daniel, Peter, Paul . . ."

"I hate that name!" There was ice in his blue eyes.

"Then why are all your children named that?" The conversation with Lisa had slipped her mind until he reacted so strongly.

"Marta named them." He changed the subject abruptly. "How about Rebekah?"

"Rebekah is nice," Hannah said. She wasn't eager to talk about Marta, either. "Are you hungry?"

"Ya, I am getting hungry. That looks like a good spot for a picnic right over there."

She followed his gaze. There was a patch of violets halfway up a hill.

Even after they ate, Hannah was reluctant to go. She lay

100

on the blanket in the sun, smelling flowers and watching insects.

"If ve don't go, ve may haf to spend an extra night on the trail."

"Is that so terrible?"

"Only if ve also lose time on the vay home. If this trip takes us elefen days, they vill vorry about us."

"All right. I'm coming."

* * *

They made good time. It was Erik's third trip, and he knew the best route to take. Late afternoon of the fourth day, they pulled into the little town, and Erik headed straight for the post office.

A letter was waiting. He tore it open, read it, and answered it at once, without leaving the building.

"What did she say?" Hannah asked as soon as they were back outside.

"I vill translate for you, but let's find a place to get comfortable first."

He checked them into the hotel. Hannah walked around their room. She had seen a room like it before in Philadelphia, so long ago that she couldn't remember it well. It had carpet and gaslight. The window had lace curtains. There was a small table with two chairs and a vase of flowers on a doily in the middle.

Erik set their satchel down and shut the door. "Vat do you think?"

"It's beautiful!" She caught her reflection in a large, framed mirror and made a disgusted frown. Her skin was darker than she'd realized. Her hair was windblown. "And I look like I should be the cleaning lady instead of the guest."

"Then look at this!" He opened a door she'd assumed led to a closet. Inside was a private bath with a real bathtub. "You can soak off the dust. Then I read you Maren's letter."

Hannah soaked off a lot of dust. She wasn't going to

101

leave the hot water and bubbles even if he had a letter from the president.

Erik made himself comfortable in the bedroom, but after a while he called, "Do you vant to hear her letter or not?"

"Of course I do. Read it to me."

"Are you going to stay in there all night?"

"I see no reason to get out just because I'm already clean."

"Vell, I can think of vun. I'm hungry. I thought you vould be looking forvard to eating a meal you did not cook."

"For the sake of your stomach, I'll get out. Tomorrow, can we eat first, so I can take a longer bath?"

While she pinned up her hair the way her mother had done it for the wedding, he read the letter. Maren and her family were settled in Minneapolis. Per had built a new, bigger barn, so he could get more cows. He and his wife finally had a daughter. Amund's wife was also expecting. He had been promoted at the factory. She hoped he like Fargo, and asked that he would write soon, because she was anxious to see him.

"That's a nice letter," Hannah commented. "Do you miss them all very much?"

"Sometimes I do. Sometimes they seem more like characters from a book I read a long time ago, and not real, not part of the life I had. I don't guess I vill ever see my brothers again. Thank the Lord I vill see Maren vun day soon."

* * *

Hannah thoroughly enjoyed eating in a restaurant. The food was good, and she pushed her plate away, relishing the idea that she did not have to wash it. The best part, though, was Erik's attention. He walked with her on his arm, opened the door for her, held her chair, and talked and joked while they ate.

"Both Maggie and Hilda haf sent shopping lists," he was saying. "Tomorrow vill be vasted, shopping."

"Wasted!" She covered her mouth in mock horror. Then she grinned. "That's the only reason I came along."

"The only reason, is it? Then tomorrow, I vill find a place to camp, and you can cook my supper over a fire."

"Don't you dare!"

"I thought there might be another reason." He reached across the table for her hand. The warmth in his eyes made it hard to swallow. There was no need for pretense. They both knew he was her real reason for wanting to be there.

* * *

It might not have been her reason for coming, but the shopping was fun. She chose fabric for curtains and yarn for sweaters and socks. She found buttons and thread for her mother. Erik picked out new work clothes for Halvor. They chose a book for the three oldest children and a toy rabbit for Ruth. They bought flour, sugar, coffee, tea, beans, cornmeal, oatmeal, some fruit, a little bit of cocoa, and a few pieces of hard candy for the children.

Hannah gingerly touched the long, pink ribbons of a gray straw hat while Erik selected a new hammer.

"Do you like that?" He had come up behind her.

"It's pretty." Her finger lingered momentarily on the smooth satin, then she dropped the ribbon. "Did you find your hammer?

"Ya."

"Are we ready to go?"

"Almost. Try it on." He lifted the hat off the rack and set it carefully over her hair, which she'd arranged again the way she'd worn it for the wedding. Last night she'd been sitting at the vanity in the hotel, ready to take down her hair to brush before bed. He'd come up behind her and tugged on one of the loose curls, gently. "I like it like this," he'd said.

Erik turned her shoulder so she was facing him. "Now the hat is prettier," he said. "Ve buy it."

Was he serious? Buy it? Just like that?

Which was better? A pretty new hat, or his words that it was prettier on her?

With a new hat on, and Erik for company, Hannah walked down the street with difficult dignity.

"Who is that?" He was looking past her. "Do you know?"

She turned. There was a troop of soldiers coming up the dusty street on horses. Must be cavalry. Their dark uniforms were clean and pressed. Buttons and rifles glittered in the sun.

They must be from Fort Abraham Lincoln, by the town of Mandan, just across the wide Missouri River from Bismarck. She'd known that the fort was there, but this was the first time she'd ever seen a cavalry troop. How exciting! This was really the West! The dusty little town with its board sidewalks and false-fronted stores took on a whole new feeling, as though it had changed clothes and taken on a new identity.

Among the soldiers there was one man who drew attention. He wore the uniform of a general, but even without the braided gold on his shoulders, Hannah would've noticed him. He must be the one Erik had meant. She recognized him at once, as would anyone who had lived in America during the war. Even after that, she'd seen sketches of him in the newspapers.

"That is General George Armstrong Custer. He's quite famous, both from the War Between the States and from Indian battles."

He was not particularly handsome. What one noticed was an air about him. He sat his horse like a man who knew what he was about. He was younger than she would have guessed. Erik's age, or not much older.

"He's the vun who vill look for the gold, hmmm?"

"Yes." It was mostly accurate. His mission was officially to scout the Black Hills that summer. They lay to the south in

South Dakota Territory. Fort Abraham Lincoln was to supply his troops. Though the mission was presumably exploratory, everyone knew there were rumors of gold in those mountains.

She glanced at her husband. "Are you interested in prospecting?"

"No. Vith the help of God, I vill grow my gold."

They stood long enough to watch the soldiers ride by, then took a walk to the riverbank. The Missouri was a bigger river than Hannah had thought. Several boats traveled up and down, even a paddleboat. The fort looked small from where they stood, and they could see troops, presumably the same ones they had just observed in town, crossing on a flat, barge-like boat. They were ant-sized from here.

Hannah looked upstream as far as she could see, which was not nearly as far as she wished. It was still broad and deep looking to the edge of her vision, and probably continued like that for a long, long way. She wished she could get in one of those boats and follow it to the Rockies. Follow the footsteps of Lewis and Clark and Sacajawea. To think it was here, right across the river, a place she could see, where they had stayed that winter on their way to the Pacific Ocean, back so long ago when the land had just been purchased from France and was still unexplored. She wanted to see snow-capped mountains, an Indian village, the ocean.

"Hannah?" Erik's voice sounded distant.

She turned to look up at him.

"You seem to haf gone far from me in your thoughts."

His eyes were so blue, his smile so white. The fond indulgence of his expression was all hers. He was hers. Suddenly, she was very glad that she was not going anywhere. She was glad to stay here with him, glad to have his children and help him achieve his dream in any way she could. She wanted that much more than she wanted to indulge the touch of wanderlust that she hadn't even known she had until that moment. It must have come from her father.

"Guilty. I'm afraid I'd gone to the mountains with Sacajawea."

"Sacajawea?"

"The Indian woman who went west with Lewis and Clark from here."

"You vish to go, like her, to see the mountains?"

"A little. I would like to see them, but I know that I don't get along well traveling. After a week, I would be ready to come home."

"Home to a tent?"

"Home to the people I love. Home to my own pots and pans and plates all in their place. Home to my washstand and dust ruffle. And soon, home to our cabin. Besides, it wouldn't be too long before I had to carry baby Erik on one of those boards on my back like the Indians use. That I wouldn't like."

"Are you ready to go home now?"

"No. But I am ready for a cup of coffee that I don't have to make over a fire."

They began a slow meander back into the town.

"I beleaf you are enjoying this. Living like the rich."

"Who wouldn't?"

He said nothing, and his silence prompted Hannah to ask why he was so quiet.

He shrugged. "I vish I could giff you these things alvays. You vork too hard."

Hannah laced her arm through his, unsure if he would allow it. There were people around. "Don't be silly," she said. "If I lived like this every day, there would be nothing special about today. And today is special, Erik. Thank you for bringing me along. I know you spent more money on the hotel and restaurant than you would have

106

if Halvor had come instead. Thank you."

He drew her arm further through his, so that she had to walk closer to him.

"Hannah?" A familiar, questioning, feminine voice drew her attention reluctantly, away from the way the wind was ruffling Erik's sun-glittered hair. "It *is* you!"

The voice belonged to Clara Pederson.

"Clara! What are you doing here?"

"Oh, there is so much to tell!" The emerald eyes swung to Erik. Hannah waited for the flash of jealousy, but it didn't come. And it seemed to her that there was something less predatory in the way Clara was acting.

A tall, blond man, certainly not bad looking, walked by with a tip of his hat, but Clara didn't even glance his way. There was definitely something different.

"Can I borrow her?" Clara asked Erik.

"Ya," he agreed, hesitantly.

"Tea in our hotel?" Hannah suggested.

"That would be lovely!" She fell in step with them.

Erik escorted them to the hotel. "I vill come back later," he said. "I haf errands to do."

The tea arrived. Clara had said nothing yet, but she looked ready to explode.

"Well?" Hannah prompted as she poured the tea.

"I just got married!"

"Married!" It had been less than four months since Hannah had seen her, and she'd had no prospects then. Hannah smiled inwardly. Well, it had only taken her a week!

"To whom? Do I know him? And what are you doing in Bismarck?"

"Joe Bucher!"

"Joe Bucher? Are you kidding?" Joe Bucher who had bought their store? Joe Bucher with the harmless, friendly face? A quiet, steady, responsible man? Hardly the type she would have thought Clara would choose.

Clara melted back into her chair in a most undignified way. "Yes! I mean, no, I'm not kidding! And he is the sweetest man in the world!"

Hannah held back her laughter. Clara had met her match. "How did this come about?"

"Mama sent me to the store for eggs. The other store was closer to our house, but I was curious about the new owner of your store. I mean the store that used to be yours. I'd heard he was a bachelor.

"Well, I thought he was handsome, but he was helping another customer, so I wandered over to look at some calico. After the other person left, I sort of . . . um . . . well, I dropped a box of buttons."

Hannah bit the inside of her lip. She could picture it so clearly in her mind.

"He came over right away to help me pick them up. There I was, on my knees on the floor, but when I found those big, brown eyes only inches from mine. . . ." She sighed, looking for all the world like a dreamy adolescent. "The rest is history."

"Happily ever after." Hannah smiled, truly happy for her friend. "Now, tell me why you're in Bismarck!"

"Oh, that. Hannah, we're going to be rich! Joe knows this Indian. He's from South Dakota, at least his tribe is. He says there will be war. The Black Hills are sacred ground, and the Indians don't like the idea of white folks going into them for the gold. He says it's really there. He'd never told anyone before, but now that Custer is going there to look for it, everyone will know. So he told Joe, because Joe is his friend, and he thought that if any white man was going to profit from it, it should be Joe."

"So you're going gold mining?"

"No! We're going to open a store! Lots of people will be buying their supplies for prospecting here in Bismarck, and we'll be here to sell them."

108

Clara glanced at her watch, took a big swallow of tea, and continued to chatter non-stop, trying to fill Hannah in on the lives of everyone in Fargo.

"You know," she said before she left, "marriage is good for you. Or maybe it's the baby. I've never seen you look so good." Pink colored her cheeks as she realized how that sounded. "Hannah! I didn't mean—"

"I know what you mean," Hannah cut her off with an understanding smile. She understood. Maybe it was the baby, or maybe it was love, but she was less of a plain Jane than she had been.

* * *

Erik opened the door of their hotel room and peered around the edge. "Is the kitty gone?"

A giggle bubbled from Hannah's lips.

"Yes, she's gone. And she's married, evidently very happily, to Joe Bucher." She laughed again at the relief on his face. She stood and placed her hand on his arm. "I believe I was promised supper?"

When they packed up the next morning, Hannah was surprised to see three new woodstoves in the back of the wagon.

"You cannot cook outside in the vinter," Erik said, smiling at her obvious delight. "It vas this or build fireplaces, and I am no mason."

The trip back was uneventful, and they arrived home at twilight, ten days after they'd left. The men dragged one woodstove into John's tent to keep it out of the weather. It took a couple of days for them to install the other two. Then the next morning they were gone, along with John, on another log-gathering trip.

* * *

Hannah threw down her sewing in restless frustration. They'd only been gone for two days. She had gone out with the men in the early morning light when her father had come to meet Erik and John, and Erik had left without so much as a handshake.

They had been so close in Bismarck, but as soon as they'd come home, his distance grew. He had work to do here, she knew, and he hadn't had any in Bismarck. But to leave so coldly like that! She did not understand, and it would be days and days before she had a chance to ask him about it.

The more she thought about it, the more uneasy she grew. Erik had never said a single word to indicate that his feelings corresponded with hers. The most he had ever said was that he "liked her very much." Was she living in a fool's paradise?

"What are you moping around for?" Hilda asked. Both she and Margaret had come to stay in Hannah's tent while the men were gone. They walked to their cabins in the evening to do chores, and Margaret hadn't yet returned. "He will be back."

"I do miss him," Hannah confessed.

"I think it is wonderful that you love him so much. He needs it."

He needed it, did he? For what? It wasn't a matter of ego. Erik wasn't arrogant, but he certainly didn't lack confidence. And why should he? He was good at everything, he was very smart, he provided for them well enough, he was brave.

"How well do you know him?" Hannah asked.

"Erik? As well as anyone in this country does, I guess, except for Halvor. Why?"

"He confuses me. I don't know what he's thinking."

"That doesn't sound like Erik. He's open enough. What is it you want to know?"

Hannah's face flamed.

"I see. It's not what he's thinking you're concerned with. It's what he's feeling." Hilda set aside her own sewing. "Let

110

me tell you about Norwegian men," she said kindly. "There once was a Norwegian man who loved his wife so much that he almost told her! It's not funny, I know, but that old joke pretty well sums things up. If Erik loves you, and I am convinced that he does, he won't be telling you. He won't wax poetic about your beauty or anything of that sort. On the other hand, he will also not tell you if he hates you." She gave a teasing smile. "That you would know, though, because then he wouldn't talk to you at all!"

Hilda thought Erik loved her. Hannah wanted to believe it.

"One think I know for sure," said Hilda seriously. "He is happier than I've ever seen him."

"Ever?" Hannah's doubt was obvious. "What about with Marta?"

"What has he told you?"

"Nothing. And I haven't exactly encouraged him to. I don't think I want to know."

"It's not my place to say anything," said Hilda. "And besides, I don't really know. I will tell you that I did not like her. I put up with her because Halvor and I both adore Erik. But don't you tell Erik what I said. My opinion doesn't matter."

Margaret entered the tent, followed by Lisa and Charity, who had gone with her. "Your opinion about what?"

"Norwegian food. I was just telling Hannah about some foods that Erik might be missing."

Hannah was aghast at Hilda's easy lie, but she couldn't confront her there, at that moment. She didn't want her mother and the girls to know what they'd actually been discussing.

"I thought with all this time, I could teach you a few recipes."

"I would appreciate that," Hannah said.

"Great idea!" Margaret said. "The way to a man's heart, you know!" Hannah and Hilda exchanged glances, as Mar-

111

garet continued, "Not that you need a map. He's already caught."

Caught? Hannah thought. *Caught in love, or caught in the legal bonds of marriage?*

* * *

The next day, Hilda showed her how to make potato soup with bacon and bits of onion and grated carrot. She taught her how to make a cream porridge called *fløtegrød*. At Christmas, she said, she would teach her to make rosettes, a sort of cookie that was a thin batter, fried on an iron that looked like a flower-shaped branding iron. They were sprinkled with sugar after frying. Also, they would make *krumkager* and *julekage*. One was another batter, this time rolled onto a hot, cone-shaped iron, to bake, thin and crisp. The other was sweet bread, filled with raisins or candied fruit and frosted.

"Most important," Hilda said, "is *lefse*. Tomorrow, we will make *lefse*."

"*Lefse!*" Lisa cried. Charity jumped up and down chanting, "*Lefse, lefse*."

"What is it?"

"Just a flat bread, made mostly of potatoes and flour, but it's a favorite."

* * *

Hannah was making a shirt for Erik. Because she wanted to surprise him, she'd gotten the measurements from another of his shirts. The material had come from one of her best dresses, which she'd ripped apart. It was solid blue and as good as new, because she'd only worn it twice.

In the evening, the last before the men's expected return, she held up the shirt to inspect her work. The hem was smooth and even. The collar points were sharp. She stood and held it against herself. The sleeve that hung down her free arm completely covered her hand. The shirt tail reached halfway down her thigh. It was too big! Quickly,

112

she got the other shirt out and spread them carefully on the bed to compare them. Virtually the same.

After replacing the other shirt, she sat down and continued her inspection. There was a small pucker where the back fit into the yoke. She started ripping, and Hilda laughed.

"He will like it! It will fit! It will match his eyes! You are concerned for nothing. It is a very nice shirt."

"Thank you. I hope he thinks so."

"Don't forget the *lefse*. He will think he is a king."

The *lefse* had been a nightmare to make. She had no aptitude for it at first, and her early attempts had been holey, misshapen, and tough. The next day she'd gotten them almost round, but too sticky. They wouldn't come off the table in one piece. She felt guilty about how much of it she'd fed to the pig. Finally, she'd figured it out. The secret was in the amount of flour. When she got one that turned out, she'd let her fingers memorize the texture. Now a large stack waited for Erik's return. She hoped he came before the *lefse* got stale.

* * *

Passop whined, then barked. Hannah got out of bed to discover what was up. The whinny of a horse outside the tent froze her blood. Indians?

Her mother slept on peacefully in the bed. She thought of the two defenseless girls in the next tent, and Hilda in the other with the rifle. But she was the one who was awake. What should she do?

In the moonlight, a man's shape came toward the tent, silhouetted against the canvas. There was a trickle of cold sweat down her back before she recognized Erik.

"Erik!" she whispered loudly, meeting him at the tent-flap. "You frightened me!"

"I thought you were sleeping." He spoke quietly, too, and glanced beyond her to see that her mother was asleep.

113

"I'm glad you are not," he added, and took her in his arms. Hannah's hand slid up the front of his shirt. She was just going to curl her fingers in his silky hair when he abruptly released her and stepped away. She felt as though cold water had been thrown in her face.

Low words in Norsk came from behind him.

"No," he answered in English. "Everyone is asleep but Hannah. Ve should not vake them." He paused to think, rubbing the bridge of his nose.

"Yon is kvite comfortable on the vagon seat. Leaf him there. Hilda is using his tent, so there is no problem there, Halvor. Yacob, you may as vell go sleep vith your vife. I hope you do not mind Ruth in the room."

"What about you?"

"Hannah and I vill take out a bedroll like the old days."

"That isn't fair," Jacob argued.

"It is also not fair to vake Maggie and have her valk home in her nightgown." With that, he sent Hannah into the tent to collect some blankets and pillows.

"Come, sveetheart." He walked into the night, leaving her to follow.

Hannah would have thought she'd be deliriously happy to hear him call her sweetheart, but somehow it didn't sound like an endearment.

Resigned, Hannah crawled into the blankets he spread on the grass. It was a soft enough bed, and he was home.

"I missed you," she said.

"And I missed you, Fog on Vater."

Hannah rested on his shoulder, but she was wide awake. It hadn't taken him long to fall asleep. He was exhausted. But even in sleep, he held her close. He'd missed her! Why, then, hadn't he let her kiss him?

Just before drifting off, he'd murmured, "*Min elskede*."

Hannah's smile was seen only by the stars. It had to mean something good.

The sun had barely made an appearance when Hannah walked to the tent, leaving Erik still in a deep sleep. Only Jacob was awake. She whispered "Good morning" and tiptoed around to collect *lefse*, which she buttered and sugared and rolled up, a cup of coffee, and the new blue shirt. Then she returned to where Erik slept.

She saw his hand groping where she ought to be, and sat back on her heels nearby to see what he would do. He reached further, then softly called her name.

"I'm right here," she said.

He sat up, rubbing his eyes, to look.

"Are you hungry? I brought breakfast."

"Ya, I am. But vy did you bring it here?"

"Because it's a treat. I hope. Hilda promised me it would be." She gave him his coffee, then the *lefse*.

"*Lefse?*" He sounded incredulous.

"The proof is in the pudding. Taste it."

He chewed thoughtfully for a few seconds. "This is good. Did you make them, or did Hilda?"

"I did."

"You spoil me."

"Don't get too pleased with me. I deserve to be punished for all the failed attempts I had to feed to the pigs."

Erik gave a long, noisy sigh. "My vork is never done. First thing in the morning, and already I haff a vife to scold." His teasing tone vanished. "Thank you for going to so much trouble yust becoss you thought I vould like it. You do spoil me."

Happy that he was pleased, Hannah said, "There's one more thing." She picked up the shirt from where she'd left it by the blanket and rose to her feet, holding it in front of her.

For a long time he only stared at it.

Awkwardly Hannah tossed the shirt aside and sat down near him. He was sitting up straight now, and she had to look up to see his face. "You don't like it?"

"I do like it. But you ruined vun of your dresses to make it, didn't you?"

So it was the dress he was upset about. She hadn't considered that he might think she was wasteful. His displeasure was more than she could stand. A tear formed on her lower lashes.

"Don't cry, Hannah, please!" He lowered her head to his shoulder. "Vat vill I do vith you?"

"I'm sorry."

"There's nothing to be sorry for! I'm the vun who is sorry."

"What for?" She pulled back far enough to search his face.

"For not being properly thankful. You are too good to me. I don't deserve you."

"No!" She was appalled. It was she who didn't deserve him!

* * *

That afternoon, Hannah sat snapping beans. There was a mountain of them to go through. Ruth was cranky, and the air was hot.

She glanced up and saw Erik coming. It couldn't be suppertime already, could it? A quick look skyward said no, so she quit working to enjoy watching him walk.

He had one arm behind his back, and he wore a sheepish look on his face. He came to a stop in front of the stool she sat on.

Hannah would have stood, but the apron on her lap was full of beans. With his visible hand, he tipped her head up. After a very short kiss, he handed her the bouquet of prairie roses he'd had hidden, and walked away.

She was speechless even after he'd gone.

Chapter 8

The Nelssons' house was bigger than the other two and took the rest of August to build. There was one main room with a kitchen area. It was large enough to accommodate all of them for holidays and other get-togethers.

Erik had built a large table with two benches, one on each long side and big enough to hold four. Chairs for the ends would wait. They had two campstools. There was still enough space in the room for a sofa and some chairs. It would have that empty look for a while, until Erik had time to make more furniture.

They had a woodstove and cupboards. Off the kitchen there was a lean-to for storing food and firewood. There was one window facing south, two facing west, and one facing north by the front door. The house faced the river. On the east there was one window towards the front, and then a door—a real door with a doorknob—that led to their bedroom. Hannah could hardly wait to get her furniture moved in. One more window faced east from that room.

Beside the east window in the main room was a board ladder nailed to the wall. This led to the loft, which was divided into John's room and the girls' room.

As the house went up, Hannah found time each day to check the progress. She measured windows and sewed curtains. She made rugs. In her mind, she pictured what it would look like furnished, with an afghan on a rocking chair and small pillows on the sofa. Someday, she wanted a real staircase and flowers planted by the front door.

The day they moved in, they had a party. Everyone cheered as the tents came down. And there were other reasons for celebrating. In the spring they would have one new calf and two foals, and perhaps also some lambs and pigs. The foals could be sold. Best of all was how the test-patch of wheat was flourishing.

Hannah made a birthday cake with a candle for Ruth, though they didn't know exactly when her birthday was. When she had covered herself with frosting and eaten as much as she wanted, she held sticky arms out to Hannah.

"Mama!"

Hannah felt her throat tighten with emotion. With a wet rag, she wiped off the little girl's face and arms, then gave her a hug.

Charity ran over to clutch Hannah's leg through her skirt.

"*My* mama!"

Satisfied with a hug, she went back to the bench to finish her cake.

* * *

When Margaret and Jacob had gone home, and Hilda and Halvor had left, and the children had been fed, washed, prayed with, and sent to bed, Hannah stood in the middle of the room and turned slowly to take it all in. Her home.

"We've accomplished a lot," she said.

"Ve did not do it alone."

There was a ring of tiredness or apathy to his words.

"I didn't mean to imply that we had. God has provided for us, kept us alive and safe. What I meant was that the worst is over. Next summer you won't have to build houses and barns and spend so much time traveling. You can break a lot more ground."

One side of his mouth lifted half-heartedly.

"Erik?" Hannah reached to lift one of his big, calloused hands and caress it. "What's troubling you?"

"It is Maren. It has been fife veeks since I wrote to her. She has not come."

Hannah rubbed circles on the back of his hand, thinking. An idea came to her, but she wanted to have a little fun with him first.

Drawing her mouth down at the corner in pretended resignation, she dropped his hand and walked slowly around the room. She let her hand glide along the smoothly sanded top of a bench back.

"Do you know what this house needs next?"

He glared at her briefly, then straightened from where he'd been leaning against the wall and turned to place a hand on either side of a window and stare into the night. "No, tell me." His words were caustic. "Vat does the house need next?"

"Beds for the children. We can use the tent canvas to make ticks, and there's plenty of grass to stuff them with. You have enough wood to make frames. But what we don't have is rope to support the ticks."

He still had his back to her, but Hannah couldn't keep the smile out of her voice.

"Do you think there's any way someone could make it to town to buy some rope?"

Slowly he pivoted, comprehension breaking over his face.

119

"And I bet that without a wagon and extra people, someone on horseback could turn a ten-day trip into a seven-day trip," she concluded.

She would think about seven more days without him later. It was not a pleasant prospect, but his grin made it all worthwhile.

"And I think someone has a son who will feel terrible when he hears he can't go, but if he's told he needs to be here to help and protect four females, he will about pop himself with importance."

"How can this somevun ever repay somevun else?" Erik asked. He put his arms around her thickening waist and visually explored the love-filled features turned up to him until his eyes came to rest on the pewter shine of black-lashed eyes.

"Someone else, I have on good authority, would give a great deal for just the smallest bit of chocolate."

He chuckled.

"She might even make a cake with it, which she would share with someone."

"It seems to me that this somevun is getting the better deal. He is a lucky man."

Her loving smile faded. "Do you think so?" she asked in a quavering voice.

"Ya, Hannah, I think so."

* * *

Black clouds rolled in from the west the next morning. It started raining in the afternoon—not pouring, but raining hard enough to make working outside any more than was necessary out of the question. Hannah felt sorry for Erik and John when it came time to do the evening chores and they had to go out in it.

The raccoon sat by the door, waiting for John and scolding any of the girls who presumed to touch him.

Hannah felt sorry for herself, too. She knew the weeds

would love this rain. At five months, her pregnancy had not advanced to a stage that made things too awkward, but hours in the garden made her back ache.

When it was still raining the next morning, the children stared out the window, watching the water run down the panes.

John and Lisa read for a while, but by afternoon all four of the children had run out of ways to entertain themselves. They grew progressively louder and more active. Wracking her brains, Hannah came up with an idea that might pass some time.

When Ruth took a nap, she withdrew a sheet of butcher paper she'd had lining the bottom of a trunk, and sat at the table with a pencil. Hungry for any diversion, all four pairs of blue eyes watched her. She was no artist, but soon she had a recognizable drawing of a small, blond girl, clad only in her underwear. That produced a round of scandalized giggles, and a twitch of a certain other, beautiful mouth.

"It's Charity!" John pointed with a squeal.

Hannah soon had him silenced with a picture of a slightly larger, underwear clad, blond boy. Then she drew another girl, a bit bigger than the boy.

They were surprised to see her take a scissor to her drawings. Once the figures were cut out, she used them as a size pattern to draw both daytime clothes and nightclothes for each. These she cut out, leaving folding tabs so they could dress and change their paper dolls.

"That vas yeen-yous," Erik said with a wink, when she sent them to play.

"Time for this genius to make supper." She went to the kitchen, wondering if she was really glowing or only felt like it.

When she had potatoes on to boil for soup, she set a fresh cup of coffee on the table in front of Erik, who was facing the window but seeing nothing. She sat across from him and put her elbows on the top of the table, setting her chin on her intertwined fingers.

"What are you thinking about?" she asked. "You look like your mind is a thousand miles from here."

He refocused his thoughts and his gaze on his wife, said thanks for the coffee, and took a sip. "My mind is right out there on the prairie."

"Tell me about it?"

He turned once again to the window. "I see more land plowed. I see acres of veat, as much as I haf time to plant, growing tall and golden, the vind blowing it in vaves.

"I see a bigger barn, made uff vood, and filled vith cows and pigs and sheep, vith a loft to keep the hay dry.

"And trees, lots of trees planted in rows along the vest to block the vind. All the children strong and healthy, running through the grass.

"I vant the veat to grow, so others vill come. I vant a town. I vant to help build a church vith a steeple and bell, vere ve can vorship God, and see our children baptized and married." He stared into his cup. "That is vat I dream for this place."

"What a beautiful dream!"

A wan smile deepened the crease on one side of his mouth. "It is yust a dream. I dream too big."

"It can happen! It's not such an impossible dream. You can do anything, Erik. If that is what you want, I'm sure you can do it!" They weren't just words. She really believed he could do almost anything.

"You think so?"

She nodded and he laced his fingers through hers.

"Can you stand it here? It's still most of fife years before ve efen own the land ve're sitting on. So many things could happen. Ve could lose everything."

A grin stretched over her face. She'd been waiting for the right time to tell him. "Erik, we *do* have land!"

"Vat do you mean?"

"Papa's land—he gave it to me! To us. He wants to open a store when there are enough people around to need one. Until then, the money he makes from his farming is his, but the land is ours! He put my name on the deed when he bought it."

"That's vunderful! But vy?"

She turned pink, but spoke the truth. "He wanted me to have something in case you weren't . . . honorable. I hope you're not displeased with him, that he didn't trust you completely," she rushed on. The last thing she wanted was hard feelings between her husband and her father.

Erik shook his head. "No. I vould do the same thing for the girls, if I thought uff it."

After Erik had read aloud and the children were in bed, he suggested a game of checkers. The tedium of rain on the roof prompted her to accept. That and the fact that she was sick of sewing and crocheting.

He won quickly and thoroughly.

"That was quick," Hannah said with a laugh. "I guess that will teach you not to play checkers with an imbecile. I'll have to stick to chess."

"I don't know how to play chess."

"I could teach you." She frowned, adding, "If we had a set."

"I could make the pieces, if you could draw them for me."

He went to the lean-to to search for a good stick of wood from the woodpile, while she drew knights and bishops and all the pieces on a section of the butcher paper.

The next morning Erik left on horseback for Bismarck.

* * *

Hannah stood in the garden, rubbing her back. Not much longer. Another couple of weeks, and all the canning and drying and jelly-making would be finished. Then no more

123

weeds to pull, no more hours in the heat over a hot stove, boiling jars. No more peeling, snapping, or blanching vegetables. Winter, as far as she was concerned, could last for a year or two.

A movement caught her attention, and she turned. Indians. On the hill, watching her.

Fear made her skin go cold. She swallowed hard, painfully, and shut her eyes. Where were the children? Were they safe?

Her question was answered by a scream. She whirled around. Four more warriors were coming her direction from the river behind the house. John and Lisa had been playing in the river. Now each of them was flung over a horse in front of an Indian. Lisa screamed, and the man slapped her hard. She quit screaming and whimpered quietly.

Hannah's knees gave out, and she sank to the ground with her hands over her face in horror. The braves began riding around the house, whooping noisily and firing flaming arrows into the wood.

Charity walked out the door, wakened from her nap by the noise. She was quickly grabbed by one of the men, and she struggled in fear. Ruth's frightened cry from inside galvanized Hannah into action.

"No!" she cried, running toward the house. "Ruth! Ruth!"

Hooves pounded. She saw the lance end a second before it smashed against her temple, sending her tumbling with incredible pain in her head. She struggled to gain her feet, but her head was swimming so that the ground didn't look level.

An Indian brave went into the house, and in moments returned carrying a crying, frightened Ruth.

"Mama!" she called, holding brown arms out to Hannah.

Hannah ran to take her, expecting every minute to be knocked down again or killed outright by lance, arrow, or bullet.

The Indians stopped what they were doing to watch.

124

"Ruth!" She reached for her.

The man holding her sent a questioning look to some-one.

"Give me my baby!" she demanded. Tears were now streaming down her face.

"Mama!" Ruth cried.

He handed her the child, and Hannah clutched her tight-ly, murmuring words that were for her own comfort as well as the baby's.

For the moment, she had Ruth, but they still had the other three. The house was burning in several spots. The tiny flames grew, licking at the wood.

Words she could not understand were traded over her. Then silence. Then they started moving.

The Indians set first John, then Lisa and Charity down. Then they dismounted and some of them began beating the little fires with blankets while others got water from the river to help put out the fires.

Hannah did not understand, but she was so relieved that all she could do was stand there and cry, hugging her chil-dren fiercely.

Hilda came running around the corner of the house from the river side to see the totally confusing sight of Indians on the roof putting *out* a fire. Her arrival, rifle in hand, renewed the tension. Arrows were instantly nocked.

"Put down the gun, Hilda."

"Put it down? They'll kill us!"

"I believe they will kill us if you don't. Please!"

Hilda dropped the gun and stood stock still. The Indians went back to dousing the fires.

When they were finished, there were a couple of places in the roof that had burned through and would leak if it rained before Erik got home to repair the damage, but the house was standing and livable.

One of the braves rode over to where Hannah was still

standing. One arm tightened protectively around Ruth, and she put the other on Charity's shoulder. John and Lisa crept behind her skirt.

"Is father Lakota?" A feathered lance point waved in Ruth's face.

"No." Hannah met his dark scrutiny evenly, trembling in spite of their recent helpfulness. She was still not certain that they intended to leave them in peace. "We found her."

A long, black stare made her knees quiver.

"You kill squaw? Take baby?"

"No!" Hannah was shocked at the very idea.

He must have believed her. He gave a jerk of a gesture, and the whole group rode away without a word.

Hilda came running. "Hannah, you're bleeding! What happened?"

"I don't know. They were taking the children, and they set the house on fire. When they found Ruth, they just stopped cold. You saw the rest."

"How odd. Who can figure them? But let's get inside so I can tend to that cut on your head."

* * *

"What made you come?" Hannah asked when her head had been bandaged and the small children were once again playing on the floor as though nothing had happened. The older two were calm, but they lurked inside the house and occasionally peeked out a window.

"I saw the smoke and heard screaming. I had some news to tell you, and I was going to come anyway. When I heard you scream, I ran back for my gun."

"And what's your news? I could use another subject."

Hilda reached across the table to hold both of Hannah's arms. "I had to tell you as soon as I was sure myself. I'm going to have a baby!"

"That's wonderful!" Hannah got up, which sent a sharp pain through her head, and gave Hilda a big hug. Then she sank back onto her seat on a bench. "How is Halvor taking the news—Wait a minute!" Hannah interrupted herself. She was so used to the idea of the men being away that she had forgotten until then that Halvor and Jacob had not gone with Erik this time. "Why didn't you bring Halvor if you thought we might be in trouble?"

Hilda looked down sheepishly. "I didn't think of it," she admitted. "Not until I was standing here, not moving, and feeling foolish."

"Well, it's probably better that he didn't come. He would've been more of a threat. Some of those arrows would've gotten father than the string on the bows."

"Weren't you scared?" Hilda asked. "Stupid question. Of course you were. What I mean is that I think I would've fainted dead away. And you stood there staring right back at that Indian!"

"I was petrified."

"It didn't show."

"I was hoping it didn't. I sure was praying hard!"

Hilda took a sip of tea. "You believe in it, don't you? It's not just a game to you."

"A game?"

"Sure. People go to church because it's expected, pray because they think they should. Mostly, I always thought, so their friends and family wouldn't be shocked. They believe others are as sweet and pure as they seem, so they try to hide their wickedness—when actually their friends and family are just as wicked and rotten, in turn hiding their real thoughts."

Hannah gaped at her, then collected herself. "I suppose that's a likely description of some folks' Christianity. But true Christianity requires more than going to church."

"So I see."

"My guess is that you must know a person who claims Christ but isn't living right. You've assumed from that,

127

that we're all like this person."

Hilda had the grace to blush.

"My father," she admitted. "A pillar of the church. Deacon, even. That is, when he's in Boston. I told you he was a whaler, didn't I?" She sipped from her mug. "Well, I have God-only-knows how many half-brothers and sisters in every whaling port in the world. Within the confines of our own house, he was quite proud of them. He would ask my brother Timothy why he didn't want to go to sea with him, like Sammy Wong. That's his son from Hong Kong. Sammy was his first mate, too, and my father would actually bring him to Boston, though he didn't advertise his identity except to us.

"When he drank too much, he would talk about the agreeable 'wahinees' and hint that Tim must not be his son because he wasn't interested in going with him."

Hannah said nothing, letting Hilda deal with the pain of remembering in her own way.

"It wasn't just Tim he would torment. He berated me for my size and my teeth. Why wasn't I as pretty and delicate as his Cherry Blossom in Japan? I don't know how many nights I heard my mother cry herself to sleep. Or why she stayed with him." Hilda's voice was bitter. "So what do you think of such a fine, upstanding Christian?"

"I think it's awful."

"Yes, isn't it? But you're different. Both you and Erik. Halvor has shown me that men are not all as bad as my father. I can even let him go to Bismarck with Erik and not wonder every night what he's doing and who he's with. But I admit part of that trust is because of Erik. I know he would never do anything like that. Erik is truly a good man. I expected him to have his entertainments after Marta died. But instead he spent his time talking to mountain men and trappers and anyone else who had been west or farmed. And he took care of his children. I was very impressed."

128

The tea had grown cold, and Hilda got up to pour more for both of them.

"I did not trust you to start with, either. I thought you married Erik only because he's so handsome, and would only put up with the children because you had to if you wanted him. But you love them. You really seem to be as sweet on the inside as you show the world on the outside."

Startled, Hannah looked up.

"When I saw you with those Indians, I realized that you, both of you, are what you say you are. And if you got the courage to stand up to those Indians from a God you honestly serve, I want to know Him, too."

After they'd prayed, Hannah wiped joyful tears on a hanky. Hilda used her apron.

"So!" Hannah took a laughing breath. "What does Halvor think about becoming a papa?"

"He is overjoyed! He even said—in English—that he hopes it is a boy! I think he knows that a child born in America needs English as a first language."

* * *

Erik made the trip home in only five days, and arrived almost asleep in the saddle. Hannah told John to take care of the horse, and led Erik into the house. Exhaustion wasn't the only thing she saw when she looked at him. The news wasn't good.

"No Maren, no letter," he muttered.

Hannah sat him down and pulled off his boots. "Are you hungry?"

"No."

"Perhaps they can't get away yet. It might be spring now before they come."

She pulled on his hand. "Come on."

Reluctantly he got to his feet and allowed her to drag him to the bedroom. She pushed him onto the bed and fluffed a pillow for him. "Get some sleep." She pulled the curtains shut. "We have a lot to talk about, but it will keep."

Even after he'd rested, he was quiet and moody. Hannah hurt for him, but it struck her that he was overreacting. What could she do for him? Nothing.

He asked Halvor and Jacob over to discuss a hunting trip. Hannah made doughnuts to go with their coffee.

While they talked, she got the children to bed, then sat with her knitting, making a sweater for Lisa. Margaret and Hilda also sat quietly, listening to the men talk. Margaret was crocheting a baby blanket. Hilda had a crochet hook, too, but she wasn't using it. She flipped it end on end, over and over, on the table. Her mind wasn't on hunting or crocheting.

Hannah chewed on the inside of her lip. Her dark brows drew together. All three of them, she thought, were thinking the same thing. More time alone. More time to protect themselves, more time to do all the chores.

Where would it be this time? North to the woods for deer? Southwest to look for buffalo? Both? It sounded like they would be gone quite a while. For all the attention she got from Erik lately, he might as well stay away.

She knew they needed meat for winter. Besides this hunt, they would butcher a steer calf. With several ducks and geese and lots of rabbits, they would have plenty. Also, they could sell the hides, and they needed the tallow for candles and soap. It would be a great deal of work, with more canning, drying, salting, and sausage-making.

The work wasn't so bad when she got a "mmm" at suppertime or a "thanks" for a replaced button. Without that, it was just work.

* * *

Hannah and Lisa were working together to make breakfast. Hannah sliced potatoes into a hot frying pan, added some onions, and cut up chunks of left-over rabbit. Lisa made biscuits. They would taste good with fresh butter and strawberry jam.

John had Charity pinned on the floor and was tickling her. She yelled and squirmed. Ruth was pounding two pots together.

Over the din, Hannah didn't hear Erik come in from outside. Ruth saw him, though, and abandoned the pots in favor of going to her papa.

"Are they too noisy?" He inclined his head to the pair frolicking on the floor.

"Let them play for a while. They need to burn off some energy."

"Papa! Papa!" Charity called, trying to wiggle away from her brother to crawl in Erik's direction, only to be caught by John and pulled back. "Help!"

"I think," Erik said in the slow voice that told the children they were in trouble, "there is a boy who needs to get vat he giffs."

John sat up, wide-eyed, and released his sister, who rolled out of his reach to gasp for air. He didn't know what to expect, but seconds later, Erik had him held down for a tickle. Charity jumped on his back, turning traitor to join forces with John. In Norsk, John called for Lisa to help, and she ran to join the fracas.

Hannah watched the flailing mass of arms and legs. Ruffles on the legs of underwear showed under skirts not kept down. Lisa shouldn't be playing like that any longer, but Hannah made no move to stop her. She wanted to join them herself.

Breathless laughter, teasing, begging for mercy . . . all in words Hannah couldn't understand. She felt left out, both by language and because she couldn't get on the floor with them. The tickle-fest gave her hope, though. Maybe Erik would be Erik again.

"Enough!" He rose from the tangled heap and sat on a stool. Panting, Charity climbed into his lap and hugged his neck. He stroked her hair.

"Ugh! Vat is this mess? Your hair is full uff knots."

"I haven't had time to comb it yet this morning." Hannah saw it as a reprimand directed at her.

"Lisa, get me the comb. *I* have time. My vife is so slow vith my breakfast, I may as vell do something useful."

Hannah's head snapped up sharply, but the gleam in his eyes told her he was only feigning impatience.

"If I am slow, it is because my husband didn't tell me he needed his trousers mended until he wanted to wear them."

Lisa looked to one, then the other, and back again, sure she was hearing the beginning of an argument, horrified that anyone would dare talk back to her papa like that.

"Inconsiderate. Yust like a man. Vere did you find this prize?"

"Let's see." She touched a finger to her lips, thinking. "I believe it was in the Heavenly Father & Son's Wish Book. He was cheap, too. Only cost a lifetime supply of pan-cakes." With a straight face, she added, "Breakfast is ready."

"I am amazed," he said through his laughter.

"At what?"

"That I managed to make it through thirty-three years vithout dying of boredom." He faced Lisa, who still sat on the bench with a totally lost look. "I am also amazed that you are here ven I told you to do something."

Lisa jumped to her feet and ran for the comb.

Erik used it, too, as he said he would, but after breakfast while Hannah did the dishes. She was thinking that Chari-ty's hair was getting too long to leave loose, and asked Erik if he minded if she cut bangs on her. It would be cute, with a braid under each ear.

* * *

"Erik?" It was evening. The children were sleeping, and it was quiet. He read and she knitted, putting a red stripe in a sweater.

132

"Vat?"

Hannah felt a bit foolish for the favor she was about to ask.

"Could you teach me to speak Norwegian?"

Amusement exposed his gleaming band of perfect teeth. "Vy? English is the language you need in America."

"I've heard you remind both Lisa and Hilda to speak English for my benefit. You shouldn't all have to change for me."

"Ve change becoss this is America."

"Yes, but in your own home, you should be able to speak whatever language you wish. Is it hard?"

"Is vat hard?"

"Learning Norsk."

"I don't remember," he teased, and she returned his smile.

"Was it hard to learn English?" It must've been a big change for him, coming to America. Learning a new language was only part of it.

"Ya. I remember vun time ven ve lived in New York, soon after ve got here. At the factory vere I vorked, a man I knew had a big slice of cherry pie. His vife vorked in a bakery, and he said she gafe him too many sveets, and asked if I vanted the rest. I knew the vord rest to mean sit down and stop vorking. I vas not tired, so I said no. He threw it avay! But I learn English gladly. It is the language of opportunity."

"Are you glad you came?"

"Oh, ya. I vanted to farm. Per vas the oldest, he got the farm. I decided to go to Oslo to study law. Then I had a family to feed, and I got a yob in a factory in Bergen. I hated it. Now I haf a bigger farm vith better soil than I could hope for in Norway. I vas forced to do vat I vanted to do in the first place."

There was a pause.

133

"So?" Hannah asked.

He looked puzzled.

"Will you teach me?"

"That's vat you vish?"

She nodded enthusiastically.

"Then that is vat I do." The lessons began immediately.

Erik pointed his thumb at his chest and said, "*Jeg heter Erik,*" then pointed to her. "*Hva heter du?*"

"*Jeg heter Hannah,*" she replied. "I think."

"Ya, that is right." He went over it a few times, then said. "*Jeg bor i North Dakota. Hvor bor du?*"

When she had that, he picked up a ball of red yarn. "*Hva er dette?*"

She repeated his words, and he translated, "Vat is dis?" and answered his own question with a merry shine in his eyes. "*Det er et eple.*"

She echoed, and he translated, "This is an apple."

"An apple?"

"Ve are pretending," he said. "I don't know vat it is in English."

"Yarn," she provided, with a laugh at his silliness.

"*Ja, jeg elsker deg!*" he said.

"*Ja, jeg el—*"

"No, dat vasn't meant for you to repeat."

She frowned. "What does it mean?"

"Ve haf had enough lessons for now," he said.

It was not an answer.

Chapter 9

Hannah sat at the table with a cup of tea which she didn't really want. It gave her a reason to sit for a few minutes.

That morning she had gotten out of bed reluctantly, knowing Erik would be leaving again to hunt. The men had decided to go only for deer, so it wouldn't a long trip, but she was in no hurry to be lonely again.

Ruth's vocal demands had forced her up, and the hustle and bustle had made time fly, as she'd known it would. Erik was ready to go before she knew it. Before he'd ridden off to meet Halvor and Jacob at the Johannsons' cabin, he'd hugged her and said he wished he didn't have to go. . . . That almost made this separation worth it.

How had this man become so vitally important to her? Seven months ago, she'd barely known his name. A year ago, she'd never seen him. Now she couldn't imagine life without him.

The baby kicked, and she put a hand over the movement. She was beginning to feel like a stuffed goose, fattened for Christmas, and she still had three months to go.

"Mama! Mama!"

John calling her Mama?

He ran into the house, tears streaming from his eyes. "It's Lisa! I hurt her! Come kvick!"

Hannah was on her way, getting up so quickly that her tea spilled all over the table and floor. She ignored it and ran as quickly as was able.

She found Lisa sitting in the river in water up to her waist. Her face was white with pain, but she didn't scream or cry. Hannah ran right into the water, heedless of her shoes or clothes.

"What happened?"

"My leg hurts." Lisa took a deep breath. "Very much."

Gently Hannah ran her hands over Lisa's legs under the water. When the girl gasped and bit her lip, she knew she'd found the injury.

John, who'd followed her fully clothed into the river, watched closely. Over and over he muttered that it was his fault and he was sorry.

The leg was certainly broken. Hannah could feel the bump of out-of-place bone. Why did things always happen when Erik was away?

John's steady talking wasn't helping anyone.

"John, would you please go get Hilda? I may need some help."

He ran off like a shot.

"Lisa, I have to get you out of the water. Use only your good leg, and pull yourself up on me. Lean on me as much as you have to."

It took a lot of effort on both parts and a great deal of pain on Lisa's, but at last she was sitting, dripping, on the bank.

Hannah tore off the leg of Lisa's cotton pantaloons to look. The skin was not broken.

"You leg is broken," she said. "I will have to push the bone back in place. It will hurt, and there is nothing I can do to help that. Do you understand?"

"Ya."

She was being so brave! Fear and pain made her eyes look like huge purple violets in the white of her face.

Praying for guidance and quick healing, Hannah felt the break again. Then she took a deep breath and moved the leg to set the bone in the proper place.

Lisa screamed. Hannah hugged her and petted her hair and back, letting her cry.

Her scream woke up both little girls. Hannah could hear them, and knew Charity would come find them on her own. Ruth could not get out of the empty trunk that served as her crib, so she would be safe. The scream also brought Margaret, out of breath, just as John returned with Hilda.

Hannah told Lisa not to move and sent the still frantic John off to get wood for splints and a sheet to tear up for tying them in place.

Hilda helped Lisa to the house, shouldering most of the girl's weight, while Hannah ran ahead to move the girls' straw tick downstairs and straighten the sheets and blankets. It would be a while before Lisa was sleeping upstairs again. And where would Charity sleep now?

At last things were settled. Lisa was made comfortable on the floor, the tea spill was cleaned up, and Ruth and Charity were having breakfast.

"Now, John," Hannah said, "tell me what happened."

"Der is dat place at da edge uff da riffer," John said, "vere da vater comes into da land."

Hannah knew the spot. There was a bend in the river, and the water had worn a curve in the bank where the water was shallow. It wasn't a very big place.

137

"Dere is a rock in da middle. I yumped to da rock and den across to da far side. I dared Lisa to do it, and she got to da rock, but didn't vant to go across. It is a bigger yump. I vent around on da land and followed her. Ven ve vere bote on da rock, I pushed her."

He wasn't making excuses.

"I didn't know dat dere is anodder rock under da vater. Dat vun, she got hurt on." Tears sprang to his eyes again. He looked to Hannah.

"Do you tink Papa vill hate me? I vas not a yentleman. I vas mean to a girl!"

He wasn't worried, apparently, about punishment. He was worried that his father would no longer like him.

"Papa left me to protect you, and I hurt her!"

Hannah wanted to hug him, but she knew he wouldn't appreciate it. To save his dignity, she merely pushed back a lock of hair. "He may be disappointed in you, but he won't hate you. I don't know if he will punish you or not. We'll have to see."

Hannah had quite a time helping Lisa get ready for bed that night. Lisa had to use the chamber pot, since there was no way to get her to the outhouse. Hannah was not strong enough to carry a ninety-pound child, and she didn't have the material or the know-how to make crutches. Erik could have done either. *Why* did everything have to happen when he was gone?

The next struggle was trying to get her into her night-gown without hurting her leg.

"It will be better when your papa comes home. Maybe he can make you some crutches, so you can get around on your own."

Lisa's face clouded over.

"You don't look too pleased with that idea. Do you not want crutches?"

"It vould be nice to haf dem."

138

"Then why do you frown so?"

"Becoss ven Papa gets home, he vill punish Yon, and Yon did not hurt me on purpose."

"You are growing up, Lisa. That is a good attitude to have."

"You tink dat I am growing up?"

"You certainly are! In no time at all, you'll be a young lady. Then you will probably get married and go away from us. I will miss you."

"Vill you?"

"Yes, I will. You are more like a friend or a sister to me than a daughter. Who would I talk to if you weren't here?"

"Charity vill be old by den. . . . Hannah?"

"Yes, honey?"

"I'm glad dat you married my papa and came here vit us."

Hannah's features softened. "So am I, honey." She touched Lisa's baby-soft hair. "Do you mind if I call you Honey? It is the color of your hair."

"I like it," Lisa confessed.

"As to marrying your papa, how else could I get a husband, three children, and a friend, all on the same day?"

Lisa giggled at that.

"Hannah, do you mind if I do *not* call you Mama? Even Yon says it now."

"I don't mind at all. You call me whatever you want." She grinned, then added, "As long as it's something nice."

* * *

Early one morning, Hannah went for a walk in the gray light. There would be few mornings warm enough left before winter. She wanted some quiet, alone, before the demands of the day.

All four children were still sleeping. Lisa would not be able to get to Ruth if she woke up, so Hannah would have to stay close enough to hear a cry.

Slowly she walked around the "yard," which was the

native grass. It was becoming trampled down, and paths were already worn through to the barn, the river, and the outhouse. She paused by the barn and watched the year-and-a-half old steer. He wasn't long for this world. They would also soon butcher a sheep or two and a pig. The sow would be having a litter, so they would have a new generation. Pigs she didn't like, and she didn't know which sheep would go, so she wasted no time on them. For the cow, though, she allowed herself a moment of sadness.

Meandering away from the barn, she bent to pick a flower . . . a prairie rose. Naturally, it made her think of Erik.

She thanked God profusely for him. He might be a little silent and moody sometimes, but he was pretty close to perfect. How could she not love him? Giddy with the wonder of it, she spun in a circle.

"I have stumbled upon an enchanted circle," she murmured. Suddenly she stopped and stared, startled and very embarrassed.

"And the fairy kveen is still here!" Erik had ridden into the yard, and was gazing down at her from his horse. The end of a blade of grass hung from between the brilliance of white teeth. His hat was off, hanging from the saddle horn, and a deer was hung across the horse behind the saddle.

"Vat are you doing out here so early? I vas going to sneak in and surprise you."

"You succeeded in that," she said dryly.

"So vy are you dancing in the sunbeam?" he asked, dismounting.

Sure enough, a ray of light sent a probing finger westward, and she was in it.

"I hadn't noticed the light."

"That doesn't answer my kvestion."

"This was here." The flower lay across the open palm of her hand.

"Flowers make you dance?"

"Only this kind." It was quite an admission. Telling him she loved him was one thing, but "dancing in the sunbeam" because a flower had reminded her of him was letting him see how much. He had never said that the feeling was mutual, though there were times when Hannah was sure of it. But she didn't want to make him feel obliged to say anything, one way or the other.

"So what are you doing here? Have you ridden all night?"

He started toward the barn, pulling on the reins. Hannah fell in step.

"No," he answered. "But ven ve got close to home, it vas very late. Ve did not vant to come home tired and irritable. Ve thought it vould be more fun to sneak in early. You ruined it."

"So sorry, sir." She reached for his free hand. "I missed you."

He raised her hand to his mouth. "Me, too." They had reached the barn, and he began removing the bridle and saddle. "Any news of Maren?"

"No. It has not been all boring, though, while you were away."

"Vat happened?"

"You should ask Lisa."

"Lisa?"

"Yes. I'll save this story for her."

Hannah went to the back of the horse to have a closer look at the deer. It was a large buck. "How did Papa and Halvor do?"

"They each got vun. They are all coming over ven they finish their breakfast to butcher. Ven ve finish the deer, ve vill do the other animals."

Hannah pulled down a corner of her mouth. It would be a lot of work, but with extra hands, and conversation, it would go quicker. It was a change of pace, anyway. And the deer would mix with the pork to make delicious sausage.

"I find myself suddenly craving sausage. Cooked crisp and brown, with gravy to put on biscuits."

"You are making me hungry. Vat is for breakfast?"

"How about eggs and hash browns?"

"Vith biscuits and yelly?"

He looked so much like a pleading boy that she laughed. "I suppose I could arrange that."

It didn't take Erik long to notice Lisa when he came in.

"Vat happened, Princess?" He knelt by her on the floor.

"I fell off a rock in da riffer." She went on to tell about the smaller rock under the water, and how her leg had slipped between the two, but her momentum kept her falling sideways. Then she told how Hannah had set the bone.

Erik removed the splints to check the bone for himself, taking care not to hurt her. She winced when he touched the place where the break was. "I'm sorry," he apologized, "but I vanted to check it. I think it vill heal fine. Did it hurt?"

"Very much! Hannah vas kvick, dough."

Then she told how John had run to get Hilda to help her into the house.

"Vere is Yon? I haven't seen him yet."

Lisa didn't respond, but her downcast eyes aroused Erik's suspicions.

"Lisa?" His tone demanded an answer. "The truth about how this happened. If you haf lied to me, you vill be very sorry that you did."

"No! It is da troot, Papa, but—" she looked down again, "—Yon pushed me."

"He *pushed* you?" He stood quickly. "Vere is he?"

"Papa!" Lisa grabbed his arm. "Please don't punish him! He didn't mean to make me fall! Ve vere only playing. He vanted me to hurry!"

Erik got back down to hug her. "All right. I von't. I vill yust talk to him."

"Tank you, Papa!"

"You are a good girl, Eleesabett. You teach us all to forgive."

Again he rose to his feet. "Vere is he?"

John had quietly slipped out the lean-to door as Erik came in the front.

"Outside." Hannah said. She followed Erik out.

When the door closed behind them, she said, "He was trying very hard not to cry when he told me of the accident. Not because he was afraid of what you would do— but because he is so afraid you'll be disappointed in him." She put a restraining hand on Erik's arm. "You have some special children."

"Ya," he said simply, and went to find John.

* * *

The flurry of work started right away. Erik left the butchering to the other men long enough to make crutches for Lisa. The patch of scrawny trees by the river would provide enough wood for that.

A week later, the women were still making soap and candles while the men, finished with their part of the butchering, were harvesting the wheat. It was good wheat, and they would save it for seed for next year. Next on Erik's agenda was breaking more sod for spring. When the weather turned bad, he would have more time for making furniture.

Hannah wanted chairs for the table, closets upstairs, doors on the cupboards, end tables, and bookshelves. Did they have enough wood for all those things? At least this work meant Erik would be around more. That in itself was worth looking forward to.

Her musing was interrupted by Passop's barking. It was not the bark of chasing a cat or finding a mouse, it was a furious alert. Hannah looked to the window but saw nothing, so she went to the door.

Three riders were coming from the east. They were not close enough to make out features, but she would recognize that black horse anywhere, and she had to laugh. The man was like a bad penny.

"Hello, Mrs. Nelsson!" Charles Cooper called.

She raised an arm to wave. As they drew closer, she could see that the other two riders were a man and a woman. The woman had a long, blond braid, the color of butter, over her shoulder.

Good heavens!

"Erik!" Hannah spun on her heel and ran to where by the light of the long prairie twilight he was replacing a broken cinch strap. "Erik! Erik!"

He met her halfway at a run, anticipating disaster.

As soon as she was close enough, she cried, "It's Maren!"

"Maren?" It took a second to soak in, then he grabbed her hand and raced back the way she'd come, dragging her. The three visitors were just dismounting when they got back to the front of the house.

Erik shot a questioning glance at Charles Cooper, but beat the other man to Maren's horse to lift her down, almost tipping out the baby she had in a blanket tied hammock-style in front of her chest.

"Maren!" He hugged her as hard as he could without squashing the baby. Then he held her at arm's length to look at her.

His grin evaporated.

"It really has been tvelfe years, hasn't it?" His voice was husky. "The little girl in the pink dress is gone! You are a luffly voman, Maren!"

"Thank you." She reached to touch his face. "You have not changed. Only the lines by your eyes. You look so much like Amund that it is frightening!"

144

"Still? How is he?"

"That will wait. May I meet your wife first?"

"Ya, ya!"

Introductions were made among Hannah, Maren's husband, Lars Strand, and their baby daughter, Kristine.

Hannah looked into the pretty face. Maren was not perfectly made, like her brother. She had long, pale lashes, one of her front teeth slightly overlapped the other, and she had a deep dimple, but only in one cheek. Charming, but not flawless, she was delightfully human instead of dauntingly beautiful. And she spoke excellent English.

Hannah knew she was also being inspected. Apparently she passed. Maren's smile remained warm. They were instantly friends, though they hadn't spoken a word to each other.

"And where are your children?" Maren's attention was once again on Erik.

"The girls are inside. Yon is around, playing vith his pets." He and Maren headed in the direction of the door, leaving Hannah to come with Charles and Lars.

Lars was not a big man, just an inch or so taller than either Maren or herself, who were close to the same size. He had sandy brown hair. His eyes were ice blue, but belied their shade, fitting well with his friendly features.

John came skipping up from the river, followed by the raccoon. When he saw that they had visitors, he broke into an all-out run.

"Hi, Mr. Cooper! Vat are you doing here again?"

That was a good question, one that Hannah wanted to hear answered as soon as Maren had met everyone, and they could sit down to a cup of coffee and a long visit.

She noticed that Maren was watching John intently. Unshed tears made her eyes sparkle. John forgot Mr. Cooper and stared back. He submitted quietly when Maren turned his head with a hand at his chin to see his profile.

"Oh, my!" That was followed by a soft exclamation in Norsk. "This makes it real. I didn't know until now how much of my brother's life I have missed!" She straightened. "I am your papa's sister, Maren. You are John?"

He nodded solemnly. "Are you a big sister, like Lisa, or a little sister, like Charity?"

"Lisa?"

"Eleesabett," Erik supplied.

"Ah. I am a little sister. Even smaller than Charity. When your papa was your age, I wasn't even born yet. But in my earliest memories, he looked very much like you."

That produced a grin. "Grampa says I am a 'spittin' image!' "

"A spitting image?"

Hannah had not thought before about the senselessness of the expression. Charles and Erik laughed, and she joined in.

Charity was climbing down the ladder from her nap. Shy of the strangers, she went to Hannah and hid behind her skirt, clutching a leg.

Maren's eyes travelled from her to where Lisa sat on the floor, entertaining Ruth.

Kristine woke and started whining, building to a full cry. Lars took her, to allow Maren to continue meeting her nieces.

Her attention back on Lisa, Maren said, "You look a little like your mother."

Lisa squirmed at what she considered the loftiest compliment she'd ever heard.

"But you are sturdier. She was a fragile bird."

That brought a frown. Two. Hannah went to get the coffee and cups in order to hide hers.

"Who is your friend, here?" Maren chucked Ruth under the chin.

146

"Dis is my sister, Root! An old trapper said he vould leaf her on the church steps! My papa vould not let him!"

"You are proud of your papa?"

"Oh, yes!"

"He was my hero, too, when I was small."

Erik was looking decidedly uncomfortable with this conversation. Maren cast him an amused glance.

"But I will tell you about my wagon and my pretend mamas, Marta and Margit, some other time."

"Who is Margit?" Lisa asked.

Hannah wanted to know, too, but she would walk through coals before asking.

"Margit was Marta's sister. She died a very long time ago."

Hannah set cups on the table and returned to the stove for the coffee pot and a plate of doughnuts.

Erik slapped Charles on the back and sat next to him. "This story I must hear. How is it that you haf come to enjoy Hannah's cooking again?"

Charles took a bite from the doughnut he'd just picked up.

"Worth the trip," he said after he swallowed.

"Thank you." Hannah sat next to Erik. "Now stop sidetracking."

"Well," he drawled, "I was in Fargo, on my way back to Virginia." He held up a hand. "I swear I was. Anyway, I was just riding slowly up a street, trying to decide if I should go through the expense of taking Duster along with me or sell him.

"I heard church bells, which made me think about what Erik had said about not going to church just to please Abigail." He looked across to Maren and Lars to explain. "That's my stepmother. Next thing I knew, I was there, warming a pew. I got to thinking about how I was wasting my life, roaming around, no good to anyone. My folks

147

didn't know where I was or even if I was alive. Why? Because the war had made me a poor man, and I was bitter.

"That got me to thinking about happiness. Who did I know who was happy, and who did I know who was just going through the motions, getting through life, putting on a good front? Most folks fell in the second group. You, Miss Hannah, and Erik, fell in the first. Why? You didn't have any of the things I'd thought were so important. What you did have was something I'd never had, so I told God I wanted it."

"That's . . . that's wonderful!" Hannah was at a loss for better words.

Charles grinned. "I thought that news might please you. So then," he picked up his tale, "I wandered toward the train depot. I wanted to write you a letter and tell you. But," he chuckled, "we all know how frequently you get mail."

Even Maren and Lars were in on that joke.

"I noticed these folks here, in the line to buy tickets to Bismarck. I heard Miss Maren wondering out loud how they would find her brother from there. Mr. Strand spoke, then, saying that once there, they could ask around. He has more of an accent. I recognized it right away.

"I'm afraid I stared at them rudely. I was thinking, what blond lady from Norway could possibly be trying to get to Bismarck to find a brother? Could it be, perhaps"—his voice grew melodramatic—"the very writer of a letter I was familiar with?"

He was beaming now. "Ain't God funny, putting me, the only person other than yourselves who knows precisely where you are, there right at that moment?"

"Thank you, Charles, for bringing them!" Erik slapped his shoulder once again. "Ve are in your debt!"

"Another doughnut should even the score." He reached for one and leaned back, pleased with himself.

"How are Per and Amund?" Erik asked Maren.

"I have a present for you!" Maren jumped up and ran to their bags, and came back with a flat, rectangular package, wrapped in red paper and tied with a white ribbon. She set in on the table in front on Erik.

He regarded it without touching it until Hannah cried, "Open it!"

It was a tintype photograph in an oak frame. It was of two men, Hannah could see. Both blond. One had hair so fair that it seemed to be gray, in the black and white of the picture. He was a fine looking man, though the other was more handsome.

She leaned more on Erik's arm to see closer. If she hadn't known better, she would have thought at first glance that it was Erik. Examining the face more closely, she could tell it wasn't. His chin was narrower, his eyes darker.

Erik remained silent. Hannah settled back on the bench, staying near him. His eyes were unusually shiny.

"They look well enough," she said, referring to his earlier question to save him having to speak yet. She added her own question. "Their families are well?"

She pointed to the man on the left of the picture. "This is Per, right? And he has four children?"

"Ya!" Maren said in her excitement. "I mean, yes."

"And this must be Amund, on the right. The resemblance is amazing!"

Under the table, she gave Erik's leg a pat. He linked his fingers through hers and did not release them.

"Yes," Maren was answering. "That is Amund. His wife and all Per's family are fine, or were when I last saw them. They sent their love."

"They have no grudges?" Erik asked. "No regrets?"

"Grudges, no. Regrets, yes. They regret that they didn't help you out. Especially Per, because he was older. They understand, even if they insist that Papa was right."

A shadow crossed his face. "Vy do they not write?"

"Why do you not write? They have made the first effort by sending that photograph."

Erik looked at it again. "Ya, I should."

"There is more news, that I think you will not like. Lena Dahl is dying."

Erik said nothing. His stony silence kept Hannah from asking any questions.

"I know you have reason to find satisfaction in that, but it is very sad. She is as tiny and thin as a child, and her skin is like paper. Her mind is already gone. She is always asking for Marta. She thinks she has only gone to school."

It had to be Marta's mother.

"Ya, that is too bad." Erik took a world-weary breath that contained no rancor. "How does Einar take it?"

"Einar isn't much good to her, or himself, either. He has been drinking heavily."

"I regret that they are going through this. I vould not vish it on them, yet I think they brought it on themselves."

"Ya." Maren's mouth pulled down at the side, and she said something else in Norsk.

"Ya, it has been a long day. I am tired, too." He spoke to his sister, but watched Hannah. She knew his specific reply had been for her benefit.

"I'm sorry," Maren said to Hannah. "You speak no Norsk?"

"I can say *Jeg heter Hannah, Jeg bor i North Dakota*, and *Det er et eple*. The sum total of my knowledge of your language. Oh," she added carelessly, "I can say *min elskede*, but I don't know what it means."

Erik dropped his forehead on the palm of his hand, which had been propped on the table, and turned a dark red.

Maren's mouth hung open momentarily before she fell into a fit of giggles.

150

"Hannah," Erik said, "I could strangle you."

Maren laughed now until she cried. "I think now would be a good time for the rest of us to go to bed." She and a broadly grinning Lars retired to the bedroom. Charles was as ignorant as Hannah as to specifics, but he snickered all the way up the ladder to John's room.

Hannah was contrite. She would not cause Erik to be embarrassed for anything in the world. What could she do to make amends, when she didn't know what she'd done? Should she just go to bed and pretend nothing had happened? No. She had to know the extent of the damage. If he was truly angry, she wouldn't be able to stand it. Anxiously she fiddled with her empty cup.

Erik stepped closer and put an arm around her. Forgiven, she wrapped her arms around his neck.

"I'm sorry!" Her whispered apology was agonized. "What did I say? Was it very bad?"

"No. It vas only meant to be personal."

It was her turn to turn pink. "How personal?"

There was a twinkle in his aqua-blue eyes. "Nothing like you are thinking," he assured her.

"Then *what?* Erik, you must tell me. Please!"

"It means, um, well, it means I like you. Sort of. That is not a good translation."

All this remorse because she'd inadvertently let Maren and Lars know her husband admitted *liking* her? It was not vulgar, it was not bad. What it was was disappointing. "You would strangle me for *that?*"

"In Norvay, it is not something a man says. Not often."

"So what? You broke a tradition. Well, it is a stupid tradition, and it deserves to be broken!"

"Sh!"

Lowering her volume to oblige him, she hissed "Good night" and went toward the ladder to climb up to the girls' room for the night.

"Hannah!" He was up and following her. "You are angry. Vy?"

She could see that he was honestly perplexed. Did he understand nothing?

"You let me imagine the worst! I thought I'd used foul language, or worse! But you were only ashamed because in Norway, a man mustn't show affection! How stupid!"

Laughing at her temper tantrum, Erik grabbed her wrist to keep her from climbing the ladder and stopped her flare-up with a kiss.

Chapter 10

Ruth woke them in the morning, delighted to peer over the top of her trunk-crib and find her parents instead of Charity, who had slept downstairs with Lisa. Her chubby face grinned at them as she chanted, "Mama, Papa, Mama, Papa."

While Hannah got Ruth dressed and changed, Erik went down. He was back shortly with a fresh piece of *lefse* and a guilty look on his face.

"Maren is making *lefse* for me. She vanted to surprise me, becoss she said she didn't think I'd had any for a long time. I didn't haf the heart to tell her that you make it."

"I won't tell her, unless she asks," Hannah assured him. "Let me taste hers. I want to compare." She took a bite out of the other end of the sugared roll.

"Good?" he asked.

"What do you think?"

"No, you vill not force me to say vich I like better! They are both good. I am going goose hunting," he continued. "I told Maren that I vas coming up here to tell you that, so now I am not a liar."

"*Lefse* and roast goose. Sounds like we're making a party."

"Haf Yon go tell the others to come over for supper."

"Good morning," Maren said when Hannah came down the ladder, carrying Ruth. The other children were still sleeping, and there was no sign of Lars.

"Good morning." She smiled back and set Ruth at the table right away, giving her a bottle of milk. She didn't want her on the floor, waking everyone.

"I hope you do not mind my using your kitchen."

"Not at all. I appreciate it. And Erik loves the *lefse*."

"Come try some."

"I had a bite upstairs. But I'll have another and fix one for Ruth. How many did Erik eat?"

"Only two." Her butter-yellow brows crept toward each other.

"They told you they were going goose hunting?" Hannah asked.

"Yes."

"That won't take long. The fields get so many geese on them that it looks like snow. They can hardly miss." The words were barely out of her mouth when the door opened.

"Ve are back!" Erik held up an already gutted goose, with the head and feet cut off. Behind him stood Charles with another. The birds still needed to be plucked.

Charity sat up on the mattress, pink-cheeked and sleepy-eyed, her hair sticking out in every direction. In the bedroom, Kristine wailed, waking John and Lisa.

"Er-ik!" Hannah tossed down her cleaning rag, not sure if she should laugh or be irritated that he'd awakened them all.

"Sorry." But he didn't look sorry. He was laughing at her again.

Maren stopped what she was doing. "You are not quarrelling about last night?" There was a worried ring to her question, as though she thought it might be her fault.

"No, we are not quarrelling." There was a warm sparkle in Hannah's eyes. "He won't fight, though believe me, I have tried. He only laughs at me."

The creases at the edges of his eyes deepened. Hannah spun him back to face the door. "Now you two go on outside and get some water boiling to scald those birds so I can pluck them!" She scooted them out.

"That is good." Maren said. "I worried that I had caused trouble."

"No. No trouble." Hannah cast a wistful glance at the door before continuing with her work.

When the men came in the door once again, they found Hannah in the kitchen beyond Maren, who was facing the table area while she rolled out and baked *lefse*. They were laughing and joking like the best of friends.

When Maren turned toward the stove, Hannah quickly pointed to the *lefse* and pretended to eat. Erik frowned slightly, and Charles looked at her as if she'd totally taken leave of her senses. Again she mimed, "Eat *lefse*." She pointed at Maren, then pressed her hands together, pleading.

Maren turned, and Hannah instantly had a wide smile instead. Erik was suddenly interested in more *lefse*, and there was a curious pucker along his lipline. Charles turned away, his body shaking with the effort of restraining his laughter.

"What is going on?" Maren asked.

"Going on?" Hannah managed to look blank. "Oh, you mean the party? My mother and father and the Johannsons are coming over later. I'll send John over to invite them after breakfast."

As Erik swallowed his last bite, Hannah made a "continue" motion. He reached for another.

Hannah pointed accusingly at Charles, and he took one, too. But when Maren looked down, he made a face at Hannah that said clearly that he didn't like *lefse*.

"This is good, Maren," said Erik. "Thank you."

"I'm happy to do it, if you are enjoying it," Maren said.

"Ya." Erik brushed sugar from his hands. "But I am full. I could not eat more."

Hannah brought the coffee pot and two cups to the table. A hard, unmovable look in her husband's eyes said he would not eat more no matter what she said or did.

"That's good," she scolded him. "You are making a pig of yourself. There won't be any left for supper."

Charles choked on his coffee and had to run out to keep from exploding it all over the table. Erik went after him to see if he was okay, and loud laughter drifted into the house.

Lars stepped out of the bedroom with a clean and dressed Kristine. "Vat is amusing?"

"I don't know," Maren replied, and arched an eyebrow at Hannah.

"Coffee?" she offered him, not wanted to be forced into answering.

When he said, "Ya. Please," she breathed easier. She did not want to confess the story. It had seemed funny, and her heart had been in the right place, but now she saw it from a different angle. If Maren thought that appreciation of her cooking had to be prompted, she would feel worse than if they'd said nothing.

* * *

Hilda brought a large plate of *krumkager* to go with all the food that Hannah and Maren had made, and set it next to the flat cake Margaret had brought. It was decorated with flowers and said "Welcome, Maren!" on the top.

156

Margaret sat by the table and held Kristine, and Lisa held Ruth while Hannah and Maren got the last of the food out.

As they ate, Erik told about their wagon trip. He told about crossing the rivers and getting rained on, and how miserable it had been in the crowded wagons. Hannah added the part about how they had first attempted to sleep under the wagon, and how Erik had bumped his head. He told how Hannah had entertained the Indians, making light of both Jacob's injury and his own part in it. His telling of the story had even Hannah laughing about the snake.

"Dis is an amazing country," Lars said. He dropped his napkin onto his plate and pushed his chair a little ways back from the table. "It is so large! Dis Dakota is so empty! From Fargo to Bismarck—nutting. Den fifty miles from Bismarck to here. Again—nutting. Dere is room for so many people. Ve traveled forever, it seemed, through hills and trees, den over flat land vit trees, now da prairie. Still ve are not halfvay!"

"You are almost halfvay," Erik commented. "I think the halfvay point is less than twenty miles. Bismarck is more than halfvay."

"And I haf heard of da mountains and deserts farder to da vest," Lars went on, in his enthusiasm over America and its size.

"Sure there are," Charles said. "I've been to Montana and Wyoming. Mountains so high that they always have snow on them. I've never been to the desert, but I hear there's places where you see nothing but sand for miles and miles."

Lars paused to think about that. "I tink I like dis prairie. It shows you how small you are in God's vorld. It also makes you closer to Him."

"I am so happy that we came to America!" Maren put in. "Not only because it is a beautiful country where everyone is free. I was eighteen when Erik wrote that he was coming

157

to America. I was envious. The adventure! I did not want to die without seeing anything beyond my village. I decided right then and there that someday I would come and find him. I started English lessons immediately."

"And you did very well at them!" Margaret complimented her.

"Thank you. But if any of you hear me say a word incorrectly or use it in the wrong way, please tell me so that I am more fluent. America is my home now!"

Erik eyed her with suspicion, then turned to Lars. "She did not vine and make your life a misery until you gafe in, did she? I know how that can be."

Hannah felt as though she had been hit in the stomach.

"No," Lars insisted. "She said nutting to me. Only to pray to God. I did not efen know dat she vanted to come to America. I tought she practiced her English for her brodder, to write. Ven my company said dey vould moof me to Minneapolis, I tought she vould be angry."

Somehow Hannah got through the remainder of the day. She was polite and did all the things that were expected of her, but inside her heart was racing. *I know how that can be,* he had said. What did he mean? Was he referring to when she'd talked him into telling her about Norway and his family? Or when she'd asked if she could cut bangs on Charity? What had he said? *Did she whine and make your life a misery?* What had she ever said or done that could even remotely be described in such a way?

* * *

Two days later, they awoke to a dusting of snow on the ground.

"Snow!" Maren was horrified. "It is only—"

"October," Charles finished. "I'd heard it could happen up here. I don't think it will last. It will warm up for a week or more, maybe a month if we're lucky, before winter really takes hold."

"But snow! Oh, Lars!" she turned to her husband. "We must go now, before we are trapped!"

"Ya."

By the time the morning sun had melted the snow, they were ready to go. There were hugs and handshakes all around. They would see Maren and her family again, but it was surprisingly hard to say good-bye to Charles. Virginia was very far away. Even Erik gave the man a hug before he mounted Duster.

They prayed together for safe journeys, but when Hannah met that blue gaze for the last time, she wanted to cry. She prayed again for him, silently. God had a purpose for him. She hoped he would find it.

* * *

Hannah got ready for bed, then went back out of the bedroom to sit and sew. Ruth needed a new dress. It was a never-ending battle to keep them all in clothes that fit.

Erik was carving. He had finished some of the chess pieces, and they sat on the table. All the pawns were done, and one knight. He was working on a second.

Hannah dumped her sewing materials in a chair and picked up a pawn. They were nicely done, but simple. Only a rounded ball rested on the tiny pillar. The knight was a different story. Hannah set down the pawn and picked up the knight. It was finely made, and intricate. There were lines of hair in the mane. The nostrils flared, ready for battle. She held the piece close to her face and inspected every angle.

"Do you like it?"

"Yes!" Beaming with delight, she swung her face to him. "This is exquisite!"

"Eksvissite? Vat does that mean?"

"Exquisite means perfectly made. Couldn't be better."

She watched his hands while she defined the word. A stick of wood moved quickly under his knife, and shavings fell into a growing pile near his stockinged feet.

"This is good, Erik! I didn't know you were an artist!"

He ignored her praise. "Tell me," he said, "vy you are acting so strangely."

"Acting strangely?" Picking up her sewing, she sat in the chair. "What am I doing?"

"Kviet. You haven't smiled for days. Vat happened?"

Hannah didn't know what to say. *You hurt my feelings? I never did or said a thing to deserve what you said?* While she didn't want to accuse him or find fault, she also didn't want to gloss over it and pretend she hadn't been hurt.

"Your silence says it is I who haf offended you. May I know how?"

Sad gray eyes found his. "What did I do?" she asked. The quiet voice she used to keep the children sleeping made her sound even more miserable.

"Do? You did nothing." He walked over by her chair, leaving the stick and knife on the edge of the table. "You are displeased vith me, but you ask what *you* did. I don't understand."

"I don't, either. I've thought and thought, and I can't think of what I did—but you told Lars that you know what it is like to have a wife who whines and manipulates."

Erik looked puzzled for the few seconds it took him to remember and think about it. "That vas thoughtless uff me," he said. He lifted her chin, forcing her to look at him. "I vas referring to Marta."

"Oh." She couldn't lower her head, but she lowered her eyes. He hadn't meant her. Relief flooded her. Then, reminded once again of his first love, she felt a new rush of grief. She struggled for control.

"I shouldn't jump to conclusions." Once again she faced him directly. "I wouldn't have imagined you to be a man who could be twisted around a finger."

"Tvisted around a finger?" He chuckled and returned to

160

his carving. "That means made to giff in?" At her nod, he said, "She tvisted me vunce, then. After a grand battle, I gafe in, halfvay. She also gafe in, halfvay."

"That is a compromise. Twisted around a finger is when a man, or a woman, I suppose, will do anything for someone. When they are always willing to give up what they want in favor of what the other wants."

"That sounds like Christian luff."

"Yes, it does." She was thinking aloud. He was right. "But the saying, nevertheless, is negative. She smiled. "Tell me about the wagon?"

"Vagon?" He glanced up. "Vat vagon?"

"Maren told Lisa she would tell her about her wagon. I would like to hear the story."

"There is no story. It vas yust her favorite thing to do. I vould pull her in her vagon, or, if it vas vinter, her sled. No story."

"Did your brothers do that, too?"

"No. They had no time for her. I didn't mind so much becoss Marta and Margit liked her. They vere the little mamas, and she vas the live doll."

"No wonder you are her favorite brother." Hannah held up the little dress, which was not nearly so little as Ruth's dresses used to be. *"Uffda,* but she grows!"

Blue eyes twinkled at her across the table. *"Uffda?* I see that your Norsk is improving."

"How could I help but understand that one? *'Uffda,* dat's heavy.' *'Uffda,* vat a mess!' *Uffda* from one of you twenty times a day!"

Erik grinned. For a while they sat, each with their own pastime and thoughts, until Hannah decided to question him further.

"This Lena Dahl that Maren said is dying, she is Marta's mother?"

"Ya."

What was it that was there below the surface, that he would not tell her? That he had said he would not wish ill on Marta's parents implied that he had reason to. And why would Per and Amund regret not helping him? Their papa was right about *what?* Did that mean Erik had been wrong?

Why wouldn't he tell her? Was he ashamed? Was it too terrible? Did he just want to forget? Was he afraid it would hurt *her?*

Her hands stopped moving. That would explain a lot.

"Hannah?"

The sound of her name in the hushed house startled her.

"Vat is wrong vith you? You sew at first like that dress is your enemy, then you stop like it scared you." There was real concern on his face.

What was it Hilda had said? He was open enough, but sometimes you had to ask a direct question.

Hannah leveled her eyes, openly searching, hunting for signs of any emotion he felt for her. She saw neither love nor indifference. She wanted to know. If he'd killed someone, she wanted to know. If he wished he could die to be with Marta, she wanted to know. It was better to know, even if her worst fears were true.

"I was thinking about Maren's visit."

"Ya?"

"You were careful to have everyone speak English for me."

He waited.

"You may as well have spoken Norsk, or Greek, because half of the time I didn't have any idea what you were talking about anyway. What is your secret?" There. She couldn't get more direct than that.

He sat up straighter and returned her unwavering gaze. "I haf no secret. Only the answers to kvestions you haf not asked."

His manner made her feel like a naughty child, rebuked,

but she did not give up. She'd come this far, chancing his wrath. She would find out what she wanted to know.

"Why would you be expected to wish ill on Marta's parents? Why would your brothers regret not helping you? Did you argue with your father? About what?"

Unexpectedly, he grinned. "Ven you haf kvestions, you haf kvestions."

Hannah broke eye contact with a guilty feeling. This was plainly not as big of a deal as she'd been making it out.

"My papa," he said, "told me not to marry Marta. He vas furious ven I did anyvay. Ve vere very young, and neither her parents or mine vould speak to us. Ve moofed avay. The first years vere hard. Her papa said I did something that I did not do. So, they said, I ruined her life. Does that answer your kvestions?"

"You did nothing wrong, but they said you did?"

"I did do wrong. I did not obey my papa. I vish I had told him I vas sorry before he died."

Hannah gave him a weak smile. "Before *you* die," she began, which made him make a short snort that was meant to be laughter, "I want to tell you that *I* am sorry. You wouldn't believe the horrible things that have crossed my mind. I should've known it was nothing dreadful. And I did not mean to sound like I was accusing you."

The stick and knife had been motionless for some time. Again he set them on the table. "Come." He spoke so low that she wasn't sure if she had imagined it. He patted his leg and repeated, "Come here, Hannah."

She went and perched uncertainly on his leg.

"I did not think you were accusing me," he said. "I think only that you resent that I didn't tell you this before. It is becoss it vasn't important until ve vere talking about something you did not know. It vas rude, and I am sorry."

"*You* are sorry? How can you be so nice?"

He shrugged a shoulder. "If it had been the other vay

around, I may have acted much vorse."

She shook her head. His "worse" behavior probably meant he would frown at her.

"Did her parents know it was a lie they said about you, or did they believe it to be true?"

"They knew it vas not true."

"Yet they said you ruined her life?"

"Ya."

"Because you married her?"

"Ya."

Hannah scanned the perfect features of the man she loved. He was as beautiful inside.

His mouth quirked, and an eyebrow pushed up. "Vat are you smiling about?"

"I was just thanking God that you ruined me, too."

"You are sveet." Strong hands pulled her further up his leg so he could hold her more tightly. "You alvays know the right thing to say."

* * *

"It is time we started some lessons," Hannah said at breakfast. It was the first Monday after Maren had gone.

"Lessons? English lessons?" Erik had a secretive smile. She remembered his one "English lesson" and how it had ended.

"Certainly, English lessons," she said. Her heightened color told him she knew precisely what he meant. "In the form of reading and writing. I believe you all already have a fair command of proper grammar in speaking. We may go into parts of speech."

"Lessons!" John moaned. "School?"

"Ya, school," Erik said. "You did not think you could roam around vith Passop and that raccoon all your life and do nothing, did you?"

"It will be a year or two," Hannah went on, "before there are enough people in the area to have a real school. Until then, you will have to have lessons here at home."

"Vat vill ve study?" Lisa asked.

"I haven't had time to think about it. I realized only just now that you are lacking in your education."

While she did the breakfast dishes, she thought about it. There were books, so reading would be easy. Did they know any written English, or only spoken? Starting at the beginning with all the sounds that each letter or group of letters could make would help not only reading, but spelling and pronunciation.

That was an area that might be touchy. How much correction before she appeared critical of their accents? Or should she teach only by example? Their accent didn't concern her because it sounded strange, but because it could confuse them in reading and writing.

Arithmetic was not her strong point. It was a subject she was not eager to teach. Before she could even begin, she would have to make up some problems to find out how much they knew.

Geography had been her favorite subject. She could give them quite a bit of information with no more than a map. Her father had a good one. History would also have to be taught from memory. Perhaps the books they read would help.

If nothing else, these lessons would give them a way to pass time in the long winter ahead.

* * *

A long line of white squares hung on the clothesline. They were clean, and it was good to see them hanging, bright in the sun. It gave her a feeling of accomplishment of a job well-done.

The baby kicked, and she put her hand on the spot to feel the movement. Her gaze went back to the line of diapers. Soon there would be two babies in them. Twice as often, she would have to wash diapers. And in the winter, it would mean stringing lines in the house to dry them.

"Hannah!"

She turned to see Halvor and Hilda coming her way and waved.

Halvor said hello and walked on past. From where she stood by the clothesline, Hannah could see Erik in the distance, picking rocks out of a field he had plowed and piling them in one spot. That was where Halvor was headed.

"He broke the handle on his ax," Hilda said. "When the head flew off, it almost hit the dog. He thought that Erik might help him make a new one."

"Let's go in and put on the teapot," Hannah invited. "How are you? How is the baby?"

"I am wonderful!"

Indeed, Hilda looked wonderful. Radiant.

"And the baby," she continued, "I think will be a boxer. I haven't been able to detect movement for long, and already it wakes me up at night!"

Hannah set the kettle on the stove and sat across the table from her friend. "You are beaming. Has something happened, or is it still happiness that you will be a mama?"

"Halvor is so happy! He thinks I am giving him the best gift. This morning, he forgot himself!"

"Forgot himself? Whatever is that supposed to mean?"

"Oh, you know how emotional they are . . . like cuddling up to a rock."

That again. Apparently the bane of Norwegian women through the ages.

"But this morning he called me *min elskede.*"

Min elskede?! Hannah was suddenly at full attention. "Is that good?" she asked innocently.

"It means 'my darling,' or 'my beloved.' It's almost as good as if he actually admitted he loved me!"

Hannah didn't know whether she wanted to whoop for joy or go hit Erik with the frying pan. *I like you—sort of?*

166

That had certainly been a loose translation.

"That's nice," she said, trying to summon up appropriate interest. "I can see it means a lot to you."

"I never expected to hear him say it, that's for certain! I chalk it up to excitement that he will finally be a father at forty-five! And I do hope it's a boy! At my age, this could be our only chance. I know he will be utterly disappointed if it's a girl!"

"He'll love it, even if it is a girl—though he may be disappointed at first."

Erik came in, followed by Halvor. "Who is disappointed?" he asked.

"We were talking about girl babies," Hannah said. She watched him pour tea for himself and Halvor and sit down, raising one long leg over the chair back instead of pulling it out from the table.

Was it possible? Was she his darling? Or was it, in Norsk, sometimes as much a meaningless pet name as it could be in English? She wanted to believe it . . . but it if were true, why would he not admit it? She had asked him directly what it meant. He must have used it only as a pet name, and translated so poorly because he hadn't wanted to lie to her about the extent of his feelings.

"You think I vould be disappointed?" Erik asked her.

"You said you wouldn't, but we already have an abundance of girls."

"I like girls," he said. "I don't care." Under the table, he reached for her knee. A gentle pat let her know he was sincere.

* * *

Hannah was self-conscious at times, teaching the children, because Erik was spending more time indoors. She started by reading to them, pointing to the words as she went, so they would learn the sounds. John was a natural mimic. If she said a letter had a certain sound, he accepted

167

it without question. It didn't take long before he knew all the sounds and was reading out loud.

Lisa was not so easy. She could not understand why some letters had the same sound, but others made a different sound in a different language.

"Lisa," Hannah set down the book. "In your language, j says y. That is how it is. It would sound odd for you to say f-jord, with the English sound of j." They both giggled. "In English, that letter says j like at the end of change or edge. Same sound. It sounds just as strange to us to hear you say Yanuary and Yuly.

"Now I know you are new to this country. I don't expect you to sound like Hilda, with proper Boston English. I'm not sure I would want you to. The reason I am explaining this to you is so you can sound out a new word when you come to one. And for spelling. If I tell you to spell 'journalism,' I want you to use a j, not a y. You are making too much of this. Some letters just sound different in other languages, though it's the same letter. It doesn't mean one is correct and the other is wrong, it only means it is different."

Within a week, they both spoke with accents and read without one, or with less of one. They made sure, though, that Hannah repeated her Norsk phrases correctly.

Arithmetic was not going so well. She'd gone through adding, subtracting, multiplication, division, and hadn't lost them. She went into decimals, fractions, and percentages. Still they thought it was easy. Hannah was getting worried. When she moved into converting between those three, and multiplying and dividing fractions, she found John's level. Lisa sat, bored, writing something on her slate.

"Papa?"

Erik had been sitting quietly, carving a bishop. "Ya?"

"If vun side of a right triangle is seven feet less dan da odder, and da hypotenuse is seventeen feet, how long are da two sides?"

Hannah stopped what she was doing with John. Algebra. The girl was doing algebra. She could not even remember how to find the area of a triangle.

Erik set down his carving and went to take her slate. The numbers flew without hesitation. Hannah could follow what he was doing, but she never would have been able to produce the answer.

"I resign!" Hannah said, then put her hand on Erik's shoulder. "Class, we have a new professor, Mr. Nelsson. He will be teaching arithmetic."

John and Lisa looked at each other with astonished giggles.

"Perhaps I know enough to teach Charity."

"*Charity?*" John was aghast. How could a grown-up be so ignorant?

"I'm afraid my education was strong on literature, history, and French. Not arithmetic."

"*Vous parlez français?*" Erik asked.

"Yes, I speak French," she replied. "Can't I be better than you at *something?*"

"Ya. French. You yust heard vun of three or four things I say in French."

"Good. I was beginning to believe you are a multilingual, artistic professor of engineering who composes symphonies in his spare time!"

"Ya?" His eyes crinkled in merriment. "I am not kvite that impressive. And you are a much better cook." He pulled out his pocket watch.

"Are you trying to tell me something?" She smiled. "Class dismissed for today."

* * *

"I think I will go visit Mama today," Hannah said the next morning. "I haven't seen them for over a week."

"So long?" Erik asked. "How have you survived?"

Hannah's fork stopped in mid-journey. "Would you prefer I stay home?"

169

"I didn't mean anything. I think it is good that you are close to them. Greet them for me." He went out to his chores.

Hannah went, though she had a nagging sense that something was not right.

Fall was well underway, and the morning sun was chilly. The geese were long gone to the south. There was ice on the edges of the stock trough and the slough in the mornings. The small stand of trees by the river had lost its leaves.

She walked alone through the frosted and drying grass that crunched under her shoes. Erik had thoughtfully kept the children, allowing her some time by herself. She walked slowly, enjoying the quiet time to think without interruption.

She wondered if Maren had arrived in Minneapolis. Surely by now she and Lars and Kristine were safe at home, and Charles was on his way to Virginia.

"Where is Papa?" she asked her mother after she sat down.

"Out trying to repair a harness. And, I might add, not doing very well. He tries and tries, and only gets frustrated. I daresay he won't sit through two winters. He does much better when there's a specific goal, like building a house, or going for wood, or harvesting. When it comes to the thousand odd jobs, he's as useful as wings on a frog."

Margaret set the kettle on to boil. "I certainly hope some new folks come next year so he can open a store and we can get back to normal. He's as grouchy as a bear."

Abruptly she changed the subject. "How are the children?"

Hannah smiled fondly at her mother's outburst. "They're fine."

"Erik kept them for you today? You are a lucky girl."

Hannah nodded at the appropriate places as Margaret

170

went on about the baby and how anxious she was to see it.

When Hannah was ready to leave, Margaret insisted that she take home some doughnuts.

"Mother, I do make doughnuts."

"I know you do, and very good ones, too. But I have more time for it. Besides, what's a grandma for? Take them. I'm sure they'll get eaten."

* * *

"I knew I had a good reason to let you go see Maggie!" Erik washed the last bite of doughnut down with milk. Whatever had been bothering him earlier, he'd apparently gotten over it.

"Did you work it out?"

"Vork vat out?"

"When I left, you were out of sorts. I thought maybe you had a problem with the farm."

"I vas?"

"That's the impression I got when I said I wanted to go see my parents."

He scowled. "You are too sensitive. I vas yust teasing that you see them so often."

He was right. She saw rebuke too easily. She looked for it. She was always afraid of displeasing him, making him regret their marriage. She would have to try hard not to be so serious and suspicious.

"You're right. I am too sensitive. I always make assumptions, and always, I am wrong."

"And," he added pointedly, "you are always too hard on yourself."

She would try. Try to trust that if he actually was displeased with her, he would tell her, and not make her guess.

Chapter 11

The afternoon was sunny and relatively warm. This was October. It could snow tomorrow and stay till May. Hannah decided it would be a good day to give the house a thorough cleaning.

She went up the ladder to start at the top and work her way down. First she put clean sheets and blankets in Ruth's trunk-bed. Her mouth tugged up in the corners when she looked at the bed. Erik had done a nice, though quick job. Straight plank frame, but sanded smooth and well-made. It still held the borrowed tick for Charity to use while Lisa had the regular one downstairs on the floor. She should, she thought, make another. It wouldn't hurt to have an extra one of their own.

She pushed the bed frame away from the wall so she could sweep the floor. Behind the headboard, there was a towel wrapped around something. For a minute she stood wondering, then she got on her knees and reached for it.

In the towel was a lace handkerchief embroidered with the initials M.D. There was also a small black Bible and a brown tinted photograph. She examined the Bible first. It was just an ordinary Bible. Why would it be hidden in a towel? Inside the front cover was the name Paul Ekqvist. A relative?

Next she looked at the picture. It was of a woman of stunning, breathtaking beauty. Her blond hair was painstakingly curled in ringlets. Her eyes were large and shining. Her nose was straight and just the right size. Her cheekbones were well defined, but not too prominent. She had a chin that gave her an independent look, but didn't distract from her other features. It contrasted with but complimented her demurely curving smile which revealed even, white teeth. Her neck and shoulders looked creamy smooth and swan-like. She was as delicately beautiful as a china doll.

Hannah felt sick to her stomach. She felt like someone had kicked the air from her lungs.

What did she have to offer Erik compared to this? Oatmeal cookies? She was as gangly as a colt, all legs and as ugly as a half-grown chicken.

The broom handle and towel fell to the floor when she stood, and she let them lie where they fell. Without realizing it, she still held the objects in her hand as she climbed down the ladder, zombie-like. Ruth tottered toward her, but Hannah walked past, not seeing her, to the outside.

* * *

She walked down along the river, unthinking, not caring how far she was going or where she was, failing to notice the black cloud bank coming from the west. When the first snowflakes began to fall, she was oblivious.

She had been drawn irresistibly to look again and again at Marta's face. Now she sat slumped in the grass, staring at the photograph. This perfection of human beauty had been Erik's wife. His first love. His true love. The woman

174

he'd defied his father to marry, the woman he'd sacrificed his relationship with his family for. How he must have loved her! A love like that didn't die just because a body did. He still must love her! Had he held her, wishing she were Marta? A thick lump formed in her throat at the thought, making her feel sick. It was more than she could bear.

The snow was falling more heavily and the wind was picking up, but Hannah sat there, numb, unaware of either. Her eyes fell on her own hand that held the picture. The nails were short and chipped, the skin dry. Her tears fell freely.

Suddenly Erik appeared beside her and sank to his knees.

"Hannah! I 'haf looked everyvere for you!" He hugged her, then just as quickly released her to wrap a coat around her.

She dropped her face to his chest with a heart-broken sob.

"There is no time for this!" he yelled, trying to make himself heard over the wind. "Ve must go!" He pulled her roughly to her feet, and with an arm around her, steered her back the way he'd come. "Valk, Hannah! Ve must get home! Ve could die out here!"

Hannah, yanked out of her near-trance, could see he was not exaggerating. Not that she would mind so much if she did die, but she didn't wish it for Erik. And there were the children to consider. Either Halvor or Papa would care for them, but to think of the anguish they would suffer—for her stupidity. She stumbled blindly along beside Erik, relying on his sense of direction.

The world was white. The wind howled and constantly changed direction. If it weren't for the force of gravity, they wouldn't even know which way was up.

An eternity seemed to pass, then Erik turned left. It became evident that they were going uphill. Then he stopped. Hannah saw tears in his eyes. He was lost, too.

In a last desperate attempt, he made her lie on the ground and used his own body to try to keep her warm. She understood all too well what he was doing, and tearless sobs wracked her body. If she hadn't been such a fool, they wouldn't even be out here. Now he was willing to die on the chance that she could make it. And she wasn't even his love, his Marta. He was so fine and brave and pure. *God! Please don't let him die! Please!*

Hannah's head was pressed between Erik's neck and the snowy ground. If the snow were deeper, they could tunnel in and probably be fine, but that was an impossibility. Even if it were a short blizzard and ended during the night, they would never survive. Only God could help them.

She turned more to the side to breathe. The storm was so noisy! Even the ground rumbled. She lay there, listening to the rumbling noise with one ear and Erik's heartbeat and breathing with the other. She was cold—so cold. And if she were cold, what must Erik be?

There was that rumbling again. No! That wasn't the wind vibrating through the ground, that was a horse! How could she be hearing a horse? She had to think. Of course! The barn.

"Erik!" She sat up. "We are on the barn!"

"Vat? The barn?"

"I can hear one of the horses! Under the grass!"

They crawled down the hill, feeling their way. When they reached what seemed to be more level ground, they went on hands and knees, trying to stick to the edge of the hill and work their way around till they found the door.

It took Erik several minutes to open it with his numb fingers. When he did, the air from the barn came to meet them in a warm draft. Erik pulled Hannah through the door and shut it, locking them in the warm, silent darkness. Then the animals started making their usual noises. Passop

176

ran over and licked them each in the face. Hannah held onto the big, shaggy dog, crying into his fur. Tears of relief, tears of joy. Tears of guilt.

When Erik had rested, he reached for her hand again and pulled her behind him into a horse stall. They lay on a stack of straw and covered themselves with more of it. Between the straw and the body heat of animals, they warmed up quickly—and painfully, to their fingers and toes.

Hannah wanted to sleep. The ordeal, both physical and emotional, had exhausted her. But Erik had questions, and he wanted answers now.

"Vy did you do that? Lisa said she thought you vere ill."

Hannah shook her head, though it was totally dark. "I'm so sorry, Erik! I didn't even look at the sky! I almost got you killed, just because, because—" Because she was jealous of a dead woman. How could she tell him that? It sounded so silly. But the searing pain in her heart was anything but trivial.

She burst into tears again, and Erik put an arm around her and stroked her hair while she soaked the front of his coat.

Eventually she was able to speak. "I'm so ugly!" she cried, in a voice that was anything but steady. "I'm too tall! I'm too skinny—at least I *was* too skinny. Now I look like a pumpkin with legs. My hands are red and chapped and my hair is straight and I look like a sixteen-year-old boy! I have no figure at all.

"Erik, why did you marry me? You are beautiful! You should have a princess! Not a—" she groped mentally, but she'd run out of complaints about herself, and she started crying again.

"Hannah!" He was laughing. "Vere do you get your ideas?"

Where was the picture? She remembered thrusting it into

her pocket when he'd put the coat on her. She dug it out, along with the Bible and handkerchief. She put the photo in his hand and could feel him exploring it with his fingers.

"Vere did you get this?"

He knew what it was.

"Upstairs, behind the girls' bed."

He was silent, and she couldn't stand it. "She was your choice!" she wailed. "I'm only the lesser of evils that were available to you when you needed help!"

"Hannah, stop it!"

"But she was beautiful!"

"Ya, I suppose she vas." Carelessly, he laid the picture in the straw. When he moved to take her hands, he could feel that she also held a book.

"Vat else is that you haf?"

"It's a Bible. The name Paul Ekqvist is inside the cover. Who is he?"

He took it from her and set it, too, in the straw. "There vas a time," he said, "not too long ago, when finding this Bible vould haf made me furious, knowing she'd kept it. You changed that for me. It doesn't matter anymore."

"What doesn't matter? I don't understand."

"You are right. You don't understand. Ve need to haf a long talk." He took her hand in the darkness. "Do you remember ven I said I vould send the children to my aunt if you didn't marry me?"

"Yes."

"I thought then that she vas the only vun who vould take all three uff them. They vere Marta's children. Marta vas alvays her favorite."

"She is Marta's aunt?"

"Ya. She is also my aunt."

"Yours? But how?"

"Slow down, Hannah. Next you vill be thinking I married my sister. Marta vas not even my close cousin. My father

178

and her father were cousins, but close, like brothers. My father's brother married her mother's sister. That is how ve haf the same aunt. Anyvay, my father and her father lived next to each other, and I grew up vith them. You already know Marta had a sister, Margit. They vere tvins, and the same age as me. Ve vere playmates, the three uff us, alvays together. Marta was prettier, but Margit vas alvays smiling, full uff life, eager for tomorrow."

"It sounds like you loved her more," she said without thinking, then wished she could kick herself.

"Ya, I did. But it vas a child's love for a friend. She died in a sleigh accident ven ve vere sixteen. After that, Marta and I became even closer friends.

"Per had the farm. I decided to go to Oslo to study law. Marta vanted only to get married and have children, but she vas alvays with me, so no vun asked her. Ve had a good laugh ven ve figured that out.

"Ve vere nineteen. I vas ready to go avay, and Marta vas sad, and said she vould miss me. I took her to a party. She vas the prettiest girl there. All the men vatched her.

"Paul Ekqvist vas there. He vanted her. I could see it in those purple eyes. Marta didn't haf a chance. He vas older." Erik paused to think. "He must be fifty by now. Anyvay, he vas handsome and charming and rich. Marta vas innocent. He vun her vithout even trying.

"He took her to Oslo vith him. That vas vere he lived. He bought a house for her to liff in and gafe her yewels and fine clothes. She had servants. Ven she became pregnant, he turned her out."

Hannah gasped in horror.

"He said he couldn't subject his children—his legitimate ones—to the scandal. Noble uff him, vasn't it?" Erik's voice was heavy with disgusted sarcasm. "He said he vould alvays luff her, but he yust couldn't keep her anymore. And Marta believed him! That I still cannot fathom. She efen said she admired him for protecting them!

"I vas in Oslo. She ran to me ven she didn't know vere else to go. I took her home to our village, to her parents. But Einar and Lena vould not even let her in the house to get her things, they vere so ashamed. They disowned her completely. I sent telegrams ven the babies came and ven she died, but I never got an answer.

"Naturally, the whole village thought the baby vas mine. Ve had both been in Oslo. All our lives ve had been together, and it didn't look good.

"My family believed me, and I know Einar and Lena did, too, becoss not only vat I said, but Marta said the same thing. I think it vas easier for them to think it vas me, but either vay they vould not help their daughter. They said I had ruined her, and it vas my yob to help her."

Erik sat up and rubbed his hands through his hair. They were warmer now.

"Marta vas in trouble. Vether it vas my yob or not, I couldn't sit and do nothing. She had no vun else to turn to, no vay to provide for a baby. The answer vas obvious to me. I married her.

"My papa vas in a fury like I never saw. I vas a fool, he said. She had ruined her own life, and I didn't haf to make it vorse by ruining mine. He said I could giff her money if I vanted to help her. She vas pretty enough to find a husband efen if she did haf a baby. In Papa's eyes, and, I admit, probably in the eyes uff everyvun in the village, to marry her vas to admit guilt. I brought shame to the family. Papa said he didn't haf a son who vas a fool. In effect, he disowned me, also. So ve moved to Bergen, and I got a yob in a factory."

"So that's what Maren was talking about!" Hannah was putting pieces together.

"Vat did Maren say?"

"Only that you had done what you thought was right, and she was proud of you."

Erik was quiet for a moment, thinking about Maren. "She vould be," he said. "It vas Maren who wrote to tell me uff births and deaths and veddings."

Hannah touched his face. She'd forgotten her concerns. Listening to his story, she was moved to pity Marta, but mostly she grieved for what Erik had given up for the woman. It was so like him, though, that it shouldn't surprise her. "I am proud of you, too," she said.

"Don't be!" he snapped, making her draw her hand back hastily. "I vas a fool. My father vas right, but at tventy, I thought I vas smarter. I thought he vas cold-hearted. I could not see then that she vas not a good choice for a vife for me. I dishonored my parents. I refused to see that they vere only concerned vith my velfare. I saw only that they did not vant to help her.

"I vas wrong there, too. They vould haf thought uff another vay. But I could see no other vay, and to be honest, that vas in part becoss I vas too proud to go to my papa and say I vas wrong. And I did not efen *ask* God!"

Hannah shrank from him. His tone, even more than the words, held a wealth of self-disgust.

"That vas the vorst. Vell, I learned a hard lesson.

"I must be fair to Marta. She vas a good mother, though her preference for Eleesabett vas very noticeable. She vas a good housekeeper, and she learned to be a good cook. She vas loyal. She followed me to Bergen and then to America.

"But she vas not a good vife. She vas not even my good friend anymore. Her heart vas forever in Oslo vith that snake who parades as a man. He created a new Marta ven he destroyed the vun I'd known. No matter how hard I vorked, no matter vat I bought for her, I could not coax her out of it. Part of her had died. She no longer talked to me about vatefer vas on her mind. I am sure there vere things she felt she could not say to me. There vere glimpses of the old Marta ven she vas vith Eleesabett."

181

While he talked about his past mistakes, he was emotional, not sparing himself. When he talked about Marta, his voice was flat. Hannah could believe he didn't care anymore.

"Lisa vas the only vun who really meant anything to her. Her link vith him.

"The only time she ever fought vith me vas over vat to name the children. That vas a big vun. She vould not talk to me for veeks. Ve compromised. That is the correct vord?"

"Er, yes."

"She vould not use Paul for a first name, and I vould not interfere vith middle names. Other than that, she vould meekly do vatefer I told her to do. I did not realize until recently how stale my life vas, then."

Timidly, Hannah asked, "Does it still hurt?"

For a long time, Erik didn't speak. Hannah thought he had no intention of answering, when he replied.

"I am thinking how to say this." There was another long pause. "I think you are asking if I vas jealous of Paul, or if she broke my heart. I haf never pondered this kvestion for myself.

"I vould haf to say no. That much is clear to me, it is so obvious. Vat I haf nefer considered before is vy anything angered me at all. It is, I think, becoss I could see vat sort of man he vas, yet she did not see me as more vorthy uff her luff. That is difficult to admit to myself, because I am forced to see vat a bad attitude I had. Who is to say who is vorth luffing? Vy do I assume I am better? I did not know I vas conceited! But, to be esteemed less than a man who could treat a woman so—that is vat hurt.

"Vat does still bother me, and alvays vill, is not knowing. I know that her love for him vas not right. But I do not know if she ever asked God to forgiff her."

Hannah waited for him to say more. After a while she asked, "Does Lisa know?"

"No!" He was like ice. "*I* am Lisa's father! I vas the vun there ven she first valked. I vas there ven she first said 'Papa,' and she meant me! She vill never know." It was not a statement, it was a vow. There would be no bending or wavering on this. "She loved her mama very much, and I vill not tell her anything bad about her. She can efen keep this Bible, verefer it is. It vas her mama's. If she asks about the name in the cuffer, I vill tell her he vas somevun Marta knew in Norvay."

His voice grew firm. "If there is anything else on your mind, Hannah, say it now. Ve vill not talk of her again."

This authoritarian was an Erik she didn't know. She said nothing, and he took her silence for agreement.

"Good. Then that subject is done vith forefer."

If they strained their ears between the rustlings of the animals, they could hear the howling of the storm, and knew it still raged.

"I vish I had tied a rope from the barn to the house, so ve could find the house. I thought uff it, but I didn't do it. I vill know for future storms."

They were safe and warm, and so far not too hungry or thirsty.

"The children must be frantic," she said. "I am so sorry! How could I be so stupid?!"

"You meant no harm. They vill vorry, but ven they see us, they vill be happy. They vill get over it.

"Hannah."

She looked in the direction of his voice.

"Ve vill talk about something more pleasant now. You." He found her face and held it with one hand on either side of her neck and jaw. She could feel him looking at her, and had to remind herself firmly that he could not actually see her windblown hair and red-rimmed eyes.

"In my mind, I see you." It was uncanny how his words mirrored her thoughts.

"My first marriage vas not in God's vill, but He used my mistakes to bring me to you. You are a gift that God gafe me. He makes all things good."

"But—"

"Don't say it. I haf heard all I ever intend to hear about vat is wrong vith you. I vant to talk about vat is right. You are ekskvissite."

"No!" Of all the times for him to confuse his vocabulary! She wanted it to be the right word so badly. "That means perfectly made," she told him, trying to sound normal.

"Ya. That is vat it means."

Hannah went dead still in the blackness.

He chuckled softly and said her name again, in a low, velvety way that made her think, for the first time in her life, that her name was pretty. "You think you are too tall. You are the same as Maren. It is a good size for me. I vould look funny if I had to bend over to valk vith you on my arm.

"You think you are too skinny. If you are skinny, then I must like skinny, becoss I like how you look."

She could not accept it. "You are just trying to make me feel better," she said.

"Don't call me a liar, Hannah. I vould not lie efen for your feelings."

"I'm sorry," she stammered.

"You hate the color of your hair," he went on, overlooking her unintentional inference. "Do you know that in the candlelight there are flames of red in it? I can thank your mama for that. And I like the vay it vaves from being braided.

"You definitely do not look like a sixteen-year-old boy. Each part of your face is pretty. They yust don't match."

"Don't match?"

"I see all the parts of you ven I look at your face. You haf the eyes uff an angel. This is the Hannah who found it so easy to luff my children and who spends her life doing

184

things for us. Your nose is like an elf's. It is cute. This is the Hannah who needs rope at yust the right time and who plays games vith the *lefse* to make my sister happy. Your mouth—" he changed his sentence to a question. "Vy do you think I kissed you that night by the river in Fargo?"

"I don't know."

"Vatching you so close, I could not help it. You are luffly."

"Then why are you ashamed of me?" It was the first thing that came into her mind.

"Ashamed of you? Vat gafe you that idea? It is ridiculous!"

"You wouldn't let me hug you when you had all my furniture in that wagon!" she defended herself. "You wouldn't let me kiss you when you came home from getting wood. You wouldn't even kiss me good-night all those nights on the trail!"

Erik chuckled, then his chuckle grew. He laughed harder, while she glowered in the darkness. "What are you laughing at?"

"You haf a very convenient memory, Hannah! Vat about valking down the street in Bismarck vith a pretty girl in a new hat on my arm? Vat about kissing you in front of Charles Cooper? That I am embarrassed to say I efer did, branding my property like that!"

She was warm with pleasure at his admission. She was beginning to be convinced.

"Then why do you push me away sometimes?"

"Only becoss I don't think a kiss should be in public."

"Why? It's not indecent! Papa does it."

"I am not your papa. I like him very much, but the vay he treats Maggie makes me feel like Ruth touched me right after she ate pancakes and syrup."

He had moved his hands away so he could lean back in the straw, but now he leaned forward and touched her cheek again. "I alvays thought you vere pretty, from the first time I saw you in the store. I vas blocking an aisle you needed to get through. You said 'Excuse me' and squeezed past, as far from me as you could get, but you hesitated, and those beautiful, silvery eyes looked up at me. I did not need to buy anything more, but I vent to get some coffee so I could haf another look at you."

"You did?" she asked in an incredulous breath. She remembered the incident very well. Even now that feeling of being a tumbleweed in the presence of a rose came back. "I wanted to touch you to see if you were real," she confessed. "At the same time, you scared me to death."

"Vy?"

"I'm still afraid of you. I'm afraid you will evaporate. I'm afraid of doing something to make you angry. I walk on eggshells, afraid that I'll make you regret marrying me."

He gathered her in his arms. "Do you know vat scares me?" he asked.

"No." She couldn't imagine his being scared of anything.

"I'm afraid of this baby. I'm scared I vill luff it more than the others."

Hannah didn't move or breathe, and she tried not to think. If she moved, the dream would shatter and vanish. He had said, in a roundabout way, that he loved her. He would feel about their baby as Marta had felt about Elizabeth. It was too good to be true.

"If I'm so pretty," she said after a time, "then why didn't I ever have any beaus?"

"I think," he said, stroking her hair, "that God sent a blindness, like a plague of Egypt, to safe you for me."

She laughed. "More like a specific delusion to you," she said.

"Hannah," he warned.

"All right, all right! I'm absolutely beautiful. You don't deserve me, but I'll keep you anyway!"

"That's better!"

After a few minutes of relishing this knowledge, utterly content to be close to him, she twisted to face him.

"Vat are you thinking?" he asked.

"I can't. You told me I could not talk about her."

He tensed a little. "Now you have made me curious. Say it anyvay."

"She was a fool. She had the pot of gold, and she threw it away with both hands, reaching for a dream. How could she want anyone else when she had you?" She touched his face. "I know what I have. I love you, Erik!"

"*Ja,*" he said, "*jeg elsker deg!*"

OTHER BOOKS IN THE *FRONTIER ROMANCE* SERIES